"Lana, look at me."

She wobbled, pivoting on wooden legs until his blurry form came into view. Then the silent, unbidden tears began to fall.

"Hey," Nash whispered, widening his stance and tipping forward until his eyes were at her level. "You're okay. I'm here. I've got you."

She nodded fiercely, absorbing the words and willing them to be true.

"Here." Nash opened his arms, and she stepped into his waiting embrace.

She pressed her cheek against the solid warmth of his chest, then rested her trembling hands there as well.

He wrapped her in his strong arms, aligning their bodies until her heart rate slowed to match his, pounding evenly beneath her ear. "You're okay," he repeated.

He pressed his palms, fingers splayed, against her back, supporting her as she worked to still her shaking limbs. Something about the embrace felt suddenly foreign and unsure.

Lana stepped back, wrapping her arms around herself instead.

Nash Winchester wasn't her boyfriend. He wasn't her anything. He was a protector assigned to a witness, nothing more.

TO CATCH A KILLER

—

JULIE ANNE LINDSEY

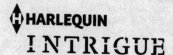

HARLEQUIN

INTRIGUE

Dedicated to the Who Picked This Book? Club

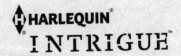

Recycling programs
for this product may
not exist in your area.

ISBN-13: 978-1-335-48958-6

To Catch a Killer

Copyright © 2022 by Julie Anne Lindsey

For questions and comments about the quality of this book, please contact us at CustomerService@Harlequin.com.

Harlequin Enterprises ULC
22 Adelaide St. West, 41st Floor
Toronto, Ontario M5H 4E3, Canada
www.Harlequin.com

Printed in U.S.A.

Julie Anne Lindsey is an obsessive reader who was once torn between the love of her two favorite genres: toe-curling romance and chew-your-nails suspense. Now she gets to write both for Harlequin Intrigue. When she's not creating new worlds, Julie can be found carpooling her three kids around northeastern Ohio and plotting with her shamelessly enabling friends. Winner of the Daphne du Maurier Award for Excellence in Mystery/Suspense, Julie is a member of International Thriller Writers, Romance Writers of America and Sisters in Crime. Learn more about Julie and her books at julieannelindsey.com.

Books by Julie Anne Lindsey

Harlequin Intrigue

Heartland Heroes

SVU Surveillance
Protecting His Witness
Kentucky Crime Ring
Stay Hidden
Accidental Witness
To Catch a Killer

Fortress Defense

Deadly Cover-Up
Missing in the Mountains
Marine Protector
Dangerous Knowledge

Garrett Valor

Shadow Point Deputy
Marked by the Marshal

Impact Zone

Visit the Author Profile page at Harlequin.com.

CAST OF CHARACTERS

Lana Iona—Small-town chef and witness to the murder of her boss and friend.

Nash Winchester—Lana's ex-boyfriend, a current US marshal hunting the fugitive who killed Lana's boss. Nash will stop at nothing to keep her safe while helping his team track down the fugitive who put her in danger.

Mac Bane—Fugitive and killer on the loose in Great Falls, Kentucky, and gunning for the only witness to his latest murder.

Knox Winchester—A Great Falls, Kentucky, deputy sheriff and the younger brother of Cruz Winchester, committed to the protection of Lana Iona and putting fugitive Mac Bane behind bars.

Cruz Winchester—Local private investigator and cousin of Nash Winchester, committed to helping protect Lana while searching for the fugitive who wants her dead.

Derek Winchester—Nash's cousin and co-owner of a PI firm with Cruz. Derek is always willing to help his family any way he can.

Chapter One

Lana Iona stripped the apron from her waist and heaved a sigh. Being the head chef at the Carriage House, Great Falls, Kentucky's fanciest restaurant, was exhausting. Especially on a Saturday night, when the place was open late and prep for Sunday brunch had to begin. Thankfully, she'd been at her best tonight, as had her staff, and she was walking out before midnight. A possible personal record.

She grabbed her things from her locker and shut off the lights in the kitchen, then made her usual sweep of the place, locking up before heading out.

The Carriage House was a part of the local history and culture, having been around longer than Lana, who was officially thirty. She'd spent her birthday working last weekend instead of going out with friends or family. Partly because her friends were all married with children and her parents had retired to Montana last fall. Partly because she loved what she did almost as much as she loved this place.

The restaurant's owner, Tim Williams, had spared

no expense in his recent rebrand campaign, and the results were spectacular. Lana was proud to be a part of it. The Carriage House had become the spot for special events, dates and business meetings meant to impress. With all the ambience of any big city establishment and all the charm Kentucky had to offer, no one seemed able to resist. She liked to think her cooking had a little something to do with it too.

Now she was living the dream, working fourteen-hour days and perpetually smelling of seared meat or hollandaise, but it was worth it. Blinking counted as sleep, right?

"Tim?" she called, heading for the hallway of closets and office doors beyond the kitchen. He'd been off his game all day, and she wanted to be sure he was okay before leaving him for the night. If she could help with his troubles, whatever they were, she'd definitely give it a try. "Front and back doors are locked, and I'm heading out, unless you want me to stay for a night cap?"

Tim had stayed late, more than once, for her. Rehashing the day behind them or planning the week ahead. They'd finish an open bottle of wine instead of letting it go bad and share a dessert from the fridge. He'd let her vent and talk through her work-related problems, until she'd gained enough perspective and peace to call it a night. She and Tim had very little in common outside the Carriage House, but here, they shared an encompassing desire to see the business succeed.

She knocked lightly, then peered through the gap in Tim's mostly closed office door.

He lifted a finger in response, indicating she should wait. His phone was pressed to one ear. The expression on his usually carefree face was drawn and dark. A long moment passed before recognition seemed to reach him, then he forced a tight smile, nodded and waved goodbye.

"Okay," she whispered. "I'll see you tomorrow."

Lana ducked back into the hall, pulling the door closed behind her. Selfishly, she hoped whatever had caused him to look so distraught didn't have to do with the restaurant. Not that she wished him personal problems, but she'd hate to see her home away from home disappear. What would she have left if that happened?

She paced the hallway for a moment, contemplating how long she could wait before it became weird. If she happened to still be on-site when Tim got off the phone, she could ask him what was wrong and if he wanted to talk about it. Returning the favor seemed the least she could do for a friend.

The narrow staircase leading to the restaurant's roof came into view, and she knew exactly where she could pass a few minutes alone. The building inspector had visited last fall when Tim had requested feedback on the possibility of adding a rooftop bar, dance floor and additional seating. The inspector had been explicit when he'd said no one should go on the roof until safety measures had been put in place to keep folks from toppling over the edge, and further testing was deemed necessary to determine how much weight could be properly supported. Tim had been disappointed to put the project on hold, but Lana had reveled in a new possibility.

When spring rolled around once more, she put a new plan into motion. One she kept to herself, so Tim couldn't be faulted for an employee ignoring the inspector's directives. And little by little, Lana had set up a secret rooftop garden.

Normally, she arrived early for work to water and talk to her plants, but midnight also seemed like a prime opportunity.

She hurried up and through the door at the top of the steps, then into the beautiful summer night. Warm air ruffled her hair and caressed her skin, while a sea of stars winked down at her. The air smelled faintly of the foods she'd cooked all night, probably knocked free from her uniform. But there were also pretty floral notes on the breeze, lifting from the flowers she'd strategically planted among her vegetables. A trick she'd learned to entice more bees and increase opportunities for cross pollination.

Lana moved to the farthest corner of the roof, which was invisible to anyone peeking out from the door. She'd arranged her pots and plants behind an array of large industrial looking structures and duct work, where the produce could get the right amounts of sun, while being kept hidden.

She set her purse down, then unpacked her apron

and name tag, along with her cell phone and keys. "There you are," she said, liberating the heavy sports bottle she'd hoped to empty today. Thirty-two untouched ounces, thanks to her wildly unhealthy routine of black coffee until noon, followed by a few sips of ice water from a cup here and there while she worked. There simply wasn't time for proper hydration in a kitchen as busy as hers. Not to mention the accompanying bathroom breaks that would result. Still, that wouldn't stop her from refilling the bottle again tomorrow. She was nothing if not hopeful.

"How about a nightcap?" she asked the plants, unscrewing the lid and making her way to the farthest pot first. Tomatoes hung heavily from the vines, red, ripe and ready to be served. "Look at you," she cooed, tipping the bottle carefully to dampen the soil of each pot. "You're perfect. You know that?"

A closing car door drew her attention, and she stood to peek over the building's edge. If Tim was already on his way home, then she'd missed her chance to offer a supportive shoulder or listening ear.

But it wasn't her boss or his car she saw. Instead, a man in a suit strode swiftly away from a dark sedan with a Pennsylvania license plate and headed for the Carriage House's front door.

According to the time on her cell phone, it was 12:10. Did he really think they might be open? Despite the empty lot, utter silence and lack of lights? She felt bad for a moment, hoping he wasn't hungry after working late and sure to be disappointed by the locked door. "At least there are other options," she said softly, tucking the phone into her pocket, then turning back to her plants. "It's Saturday night in Great Falls. A half dozen honky-tonks are probably serving wings and beer for another two hours." She smiled as she divvied up the rest of her water, suddenly tuned in to the distant sounds of country music a block or two away.

"Wow." Lana sighed, admiring her fat green peppers. "I am thirty, single and talking to plants after midnight. Maybe it's time I adopt a half dozen cats and own my future."

A thunder of angry voices rose beneath her feet, stilling her body and cooling her smile. Tim's unmistakable tenor mixed with a heated, less Southern-leaning bass, and together they sounded like war.

Lana recapped the water bottle, then crept toward the door to the stairs, straining to understand the argument or at least identify the second voice. Had someone come in through the back? Or was it the man in the suit who'd just arrived? She peered cautiously over the roof's edge once more, surprised to see the car hadn't moved.

Could Tim have a friend visiting from Pennsylvania?

The echo of feet on wooden steps reached her ears before she made it to the door.

She scurried back, afraid of being caught where she didn't belong and embarrassed for obviously overhearing their fight, even if she hadn't been able to make out a word of it.

The door swung open hard, as if kicked or intentionally thrown, and it smacked against the wall.

Lana scrambled farther into the shadows, ducking behind the metal boxes and pipes. She eyeballed the fire escape near her plants as a possibly necessary exit.

"It's not what you think," Tim said, an unnatural strain in his usually jovial voice. The heat from moments before had thoroughly gone. "You've got it all wrong. I can explain."

"I told you," the other man replied, his tone eerily calm. "I'm not here for an explanation. We already know what you did."

Lana's muscles tensed painfully. Had this man just made a threat? Is this what Tim had been so upset about all day? What could her easygoing boss have done to cause anyone to speak to him that way?

And if the second guy hadn't come for an explanation, then what had he come for?

"I'm sorry," Tim said, his voice sliding from strained to panicked. "I didn't mean to overstep. We were just fooling around. Having some fun. It was all an honest mistake."

"It was a mistake," the other man said. "But not an honest one, and not the kind that can be overlooked or forgiven. It's bad for business. And it's my job to send a clear message when something like this comes to light."

"No," Tim said, breathless.

His desperation sent icy prickles over Lana's arms

and down her spine. Her heart pounded, and her ears began to ring. She needed to do something, but what? Pop out and announce herself? Would that break the tension or make it worse? Should she call the police? What would she say? And if Tim was involved with something he shouldn't be, would her call result in his arrest?

Could her attempt to help do more harm than good?

She willed her feet to move and prepared to step into view. With luck, her presence would be enough to at least put a pin in their conversation. Maybe she could cause them to table it for another time.

She counted down from three, then stepped into view.

The man's back was to her, and Tim spotted her immediately from his position at the roof's edge. He shook his head hard in warning, she thought, and she inched back out of sight.

The sound of a gun's hammer being drawn sent her heart into her throat.

She clamped a hand across her mouth as she peeked around the corner once more, this time careful to remain hidden. She watched in horror as the man raised a gun to Tim's face. Then, like the terrified person she was, she ran.

Her feet were over the roof's edge and planted soundly against the fire escape's top rung before her next coherent thought could register. She'd grabbed her purse and dropped it over her head, cross-body, to free her hands on the rails, and she'd left everything, including sanity and caution, behind. All she could do now was dial 9-1-1 the moment her feet hit the ground.

Across the rooftop, a scream split the air, growing briefly louder before ending with a muffled thump.

Lana gasped, and a strangled cry escaped as her eyes blurred with tears. The screech of tires and explosion of voices indicated there were at least witnesses to Tim's fall, if that was what had happened.

Maybe he'd turned the situation around, gotten the best of his attacker. She could attest to the gun and the threat. She was there, and there were other witnesses too. She wouldn't be alone in her tale.

Heavy footfalls crossed the rooftop in her direction as she continued toward the ground, holding on to hope that somehow she was wrong about everything and no one had died. She glanced instinctively at the broken pavement below, still another six, maybe eight, feet away. Her sweat-slicked palms slid on the rails, causing the ladder to rattle and shake. Then, with an image of the killer's gun in her mind, she pushed off the fire escape and leaped to the ground.

Her body hit with a reverberating thud, sending her into a roll that landed her momentarily on her back. The twisted, angry face of Tim's killer came into view on the roof looking down, her forgotten apron and name badge gripped in one meaty hand.

Chapter Two

Nash Winchester attempted to rub the fatigue from his eyes, as the dark country road before him began to blur. He'd been awake far longer than anyone should be, and he was still a few miles outside his destination of Great Falls, Kentucky. The small country town was home to his extended family, plenty of high school friends and, according to his best criminal informant, a fugitive named Mac Bane. Nash and his team at the US Marshals had been chasing Bane for well over a year, and if this tip panned out, it would be the closest they'd been to nabbing him.

He powered down his window, trading the truck's subtle air conditioning for the whipping night wind. It was already after midnight, and the sooner he reached the local sheriff's department the better. He needed to brief his cousin, Knox, and the other deputies on Bane's presence, known affiliates and patterns of behavior. The sooner local authorities understood who and what they were looking for, the sooner they could assist in the fugitive's apprehension.

Nash slowed at the last stoplight outside town, waiting impatiently for the signal to change. A list of Bane's crimes, both known and suspected, raced through his mind, long and fast as a freight train. Hunting this man was Nash's job, but it had become his life's purpose these last few months as well. He'd been immersed in the details and history of the criminal and considered himself an expert on the subject. Which was why he'd hit the road as soon as his informant had claimed Bane was in Great Falls. If it was true, Nash would know within a day or two. Bane's ties to illegal gambling and money laundering were deep, and small towns were a great way to turn a profit, then cover the crimes quickly, while flying under the radar. But this particular small town was Nash's old stomping ground. He'd lived there for four years following his service in the military, and anything he didn't know about the community from his time there his family would.

Mac Bane had chosen the wrong area to corrupt this time, and it would be his downfall.

The Great Falls sign appeared beneath a streetlamp on Nash's right, and nostalgia hit like a ramrod to the chest. Wonder widened his tired eyes and sat him straighter in his seat. He hadn't been back in eight years, and the idea of setting eyes on the place again had him straining against the darkness.

Main Street formed up ahead, and he pressed the accelerator with new purpose, eager to revisit the streets he'd roamed during family visits as a kid, on military leave and with the woman who haunted his dreams. Nash had made a lot of incredible memories in Great Falls. He cared deeply for the people and the town. Leaving without Bane wouldn't be an option.

Nash slowed to take in the sights and sounds of a louder, livelier downtown than he recalled. Cowboys and country girls spilled from the open doors of honky-tonks, dancing and laughing on the sidewalks and in the street. Strings of white bistro lights hung in swoops overhead, and wooden barricades had been erected at each corner to protect pedestrians in the area. It was nothing like life in Louisville, where entertainment was ongoing and nightly, but businesses like these were exactly the sorts of places gambling and money laundering were proven to thrive.

He debated parking and getting an immediate start on his hunt for Bane, but Nash was running late, and his cousin Knox's shift was ending soon.

Reluctantly, he engaged his turn signal, then made the final turn toward the Great Falls Sheriff's Department, only a few miles up the road. He was just in time to see Knox and another deputy heading for a pair of cruisers parked outside.

"Hey," Nash called, pulling alongside Knox. "Headed home?" he asked, double-checking the clock on his dashboard.

"No." Knox shook his head and offered his hand for a shake. "It's good to see you, but my shift just got a lot longer. This call is going to keep me busy for a while. You can go on over to my place, if you want. Get some food and a little sleep. We can talk to the rest of the department first thing in the morning."

"What's the call?" Nash asked, intuition tugging at his skin.

"Possible jumper over at the Carriage House," Knox said, stepping backward, toward his cruiser. He raised a hand in parting to the man he'd walked into the lot with. "Witnesses saw the man fall. He didn't get up."

The other deputy dropped into a waiting cruiser and pulled away, lights flashing.

"The Carriage House?" Nash asked, unfamiliar with the name.

"Yeah. Nice place. It was an Italian restaurant when we were kids."

Nash nodded, a phantom fist tightening in his chest. The woman of his dreams had been addicted to the gnocchi, and he'd taken her there every chance he'd gotten while he lived in this town.

Before he'd stupidly broken both of their hearts.

"You're welcome to tag along," Knox said, moving slowly away from Nash's ride. "But I've got to roll."

"All right," he said. "Any chance the Carriage House got a high-end makeover in the last twelve to twenty-four months?"

Knox frowned. "Yeah, it and half the businesses in the area. City council's been passing levies and revitalizing downtown, in case you didn't notice on your way in." He stuffed his big deputy hat onto his head and turned away. "I'll meet you there."

Nash waited while Knox reversed from his parking spot then headed into the night. He kept pace at his cousin's bumper, letting his mind wander as they drove. He mentally tallied the odds that someone fell from the roof of a newly upgraded business in a town where Bane had recently arrived and the death was unrelated. More likely, Nash thought, the jumper had help finding his way over the edge.

He parked at the end of the block, several yards away from Knox's cruiser and the crowd. Then he took a beat to observe the emergency crews, lights and hubbub.

Crime-scene tape had been strung around the perimeter, pushing people back and causing them to gather in knots and clusters along it. An ambulance blocked Nash's view of the unlucky faller at the center of the scene.

Knox ejected from the cruiser a moment later and marched into the mix, shoulders square. It was too late to help the victim now, but it was never too late for justice.

Nash stretched his neck and rolled his shoulders, then scanned the area for signs of someone a little too interested in the crime scene. It took less than thirty seconds to spot a figure in a dark hoodie, slowly pacing the periphery. The person shifted from foot to foot, clearly anxious, as they made their way closer to the authorities working the scene.

Nash opened his door and slipped silently to his feet. He tugged a ball cap low on his head and hunched his shoulders to diminish his height and conceal his presence. Right now, he needed to blend in. If he managed to get the hooded figure alone, he might be able to shake loose some useful information. When Nash paired his badge with his practiced tough-guy expression, it greased a lot of tight lips. He doubted the person in the hoodie would be any different, and based on the anxious looks they were throwing over each shoulder, Hoodie knew something worth telling.

Knox's head lifted as Nash drew near, brow furrowed in curiosity.

He shot a pointed look at the person in question, then waited as Knox tracked his gaze.

The hooded figure spun suddenly, as if Nash's silent approach had been broadcast by a bullhorn. Their shadow-cloaked face jerked in Nash's direction, a half heartbeat before they broke into a run.

"Dang it," Nash complained. He was too darn tired to sprint, but his person of interest was getting away. "Stop!" he called, mustering all the authority he could manage, without shouting his credentials. It wasn't the time to announce his presence in Great Falls, in case Bane or his lackeys got word. The advantage of surprise was all Nash had going for him.

A distinctly feminine shape became clearer as Hoodie passed through a swath of light. Her every heaved breath and sway of gently curved hips removed all possibilities Nash was chasing a male.

But why did the mysterious figure suddenly feel so achingly familiar?

She skidded around the back of the building, and Nash pushed into high gear, rounding the same corner three long strides later.

A winding blast to his gut sent air whooshing from his lungs.

Hoodie tossed her broken slat of wood aside, and it clattered to the ground. Then she escaped anew.

"Great Falls Sheriff's Department," Knox announced. His distant voice boomed through the night, the words infused with enough authority to stop a freight train.

Thank goodness for smart lawmen and backup.

Nash forced himself upright, taking shallow sips of air as the runner closed the distance to Knox's side without stopping.

She spun back as she reached his cousin, one arm flung out, a finger pointed in Nash's direction. "Help! That man is chasing me!" The hood fell away as she cried, revealing the face of an angel. A face he'd known intimately once, and one he'd seen every time he'd closed his eyes for the past eight years.

Lana Iona.

Chapter Three

Lana's already-racing heart broke into a sprint as she stood, speechless, between the two towering Winchesters. She'd never been as relieved as she'd felt when the familiar deputy stepped into her path, intercepting and saving her from the hulking figure at her back. It'd taken all the bravery she'd had to stop running and defend herself a few moments before.

The memory of wielding a broken board and of the bone-jarring impact it had made against her assailant's core returned with a shock, and her ears rang in horror.

The man hadn't been an assailant. He was Nash Winchester, someone she hadn't seen in eight years, since the day he'd stolen, then run off with, her young heart.

"I am so sorry," she blurted, mind spinning and stomach churning. "Did I hurt you?"

Knox gave a short chuckle at her back. "Yeah, Nash. Did she hurt you?"

Nash narrowed his eyes. He dropped the massive palm away from his middle and glared. "I'm fine. Though I don't understand what you're doing here," he grouched, sliding his heated gaze to Lana. "I thought I was chasing a killer, or at least a witness who'd known enough to take off, rather than tattle on Mac Bane."

"Who's Mac Bane?" she asked. The memory of the man who'd killed Tim burst back to mind. "Is he from Pennsylvania?"

Nash cocked a hip and lifted a brow, analyzing her as she squirmed beneath his scrutiny. "Yeah. How did you know that? And why were you running from me?"

She'd run because he'd given chase, and she had no reason to think a good guy would do that. She'd only finished running from a killer a few minutes before.

Then a hulking figure had risen from a dark SUV at the curb and headed for her. What was she supposed to do? Stick around and make acquaintances? "I didn't know it was you," she said simply. "Why did you chase me?"

"Because you ran."

"Well, I ran because you chased me," she snapped.

He made a throaty, humorless sound of disbelief, and a rush of emotion clogged her throat and stung her eyes.

To her dismay, Nash hadn't changed much in the years since she'd last seen him, though he'd become impossibly, unfairly, better-looking. He'd been twenty-two and fresh from the military when they'd met, with short hair and long, ropey limbs. The man before her now looked every bit of thirty-four, with wider shoulders and a broader chest. His dramatically square jawline and imposing height seemed more remarkable and less awkward. In a word, he was gorgeous.

And she looked like a train wreck.

Lana ran an anxious hand over her fuzzy hair, tangled by the static and friction from her hood. She hated that her clothes smelled of her restaurant's kitchen and that her makeup had been washed away by tears. More than that, she hated herself for caring about her appearance, or what anyone thought of it, when her boss lay dead on the other side of the building.

Nash shifted, scanning the night around them. "How'd you know Bane was from Pennsylvania?" he asked, circling back to an earlier question.

"I saw the plates on the car," she said, absently, her whirring thoughts struggling to find purchase. "I don't understand what you're doing here."

She rubbed her throbbing forehead, unable to make sense of anything that had happened since she'd gone to water her plants. "You left. You don't live here anymore." Her hand fell away, and she stared into his deep blue eyes. Two hours ago, it had been a normal day. "What's going on?"

Knox moved to her side, startling her. She'd been so rapt with Nash, she'd nearly forgotten his cousin was there. "Nash is here on US Marshal business," he explained. "He's looking for a fugitive by the name of Mac Bane, and it seems like you might've found him."

Nash's eyes flashed, rising from Lana's gaze to Knox's before falling back to meet hers.

Knox reached across the space and set a hand briefly on his cousin's shoulder, lips quirked into a humorless smile. "And you thought it could take days to prove or disprove your intel. Looks like tonight's your lucky night. You found yourself an eyewitness. And one you know you can trust."

Lana changed the angle of her stance, forming a small triangle with the men. She looked from one Winchester to the other, attempting to piece the jumble of information together. "You're looking for a fugitive?" she asked Nash. "And based on the timing of Tim's..." She shook her head, unable to speak any of the words coming quickly to mind—*death, murder, fall*—and swallowed hard and tried again. "You think the man I saw, whose car had Pennsylvania plates, could be your guy?"

Nash nodded. "That's right. And if you got a look at him, there's a good chance he saw you too."

"He absolutely did," she said, recalling the killer's scowling, deranged face with toe-curling clarity.

"Winchester!" a new voice called from the corner of the building.

Lana's little group turned in near unison to see who was there.

A deputy waved one arm overhead, beckoning Knox, she supposed, though he could've meant to call either man or both.

"Yeah." Knox lifted a hand in acknowledgment, then turned his eyes to Lana. "I need your full statement, in writing. And I'd prefer you to give it at the sheriff's department. I've got to—"

"I'll take her," Nash said, not bothering to wait for whatever else his cousin planned to say. "We'll head out now, and I'll stay with her until you get there."

Knox furrowed his brow but didn't argue. "Lana?" he asked. "That okay with you?"

She nodded woodenly, the heavy reality of the bigger picture returning like an anvil. She'd seen her friend murdered tonight, then looked into his killer's eyes. And now she had to relive it. She had to speak the words, then write them down. All so a fugitive could be stopped before he hurt someone else. Maybe even her.

Knox dipped his chin in agreement. "I'll finish up here, then head over. We'll try to get you home as soon as we can."

Lana's arms began to tremble, and she wrapped them around her center, unable to think of going home. "He saw my face," she said, freezing both men in place. "And he has my apron and name tag. I left them on the roof."

Nash made a low, guttural sound, then fixed her with a heated stare. "You're not going home for a while, then. We can talk about the details on the road."

Her mouth fell open, but she didn't argue. The expression on his face and the twist in her gut said not to bother. Nash was right. It wouldn't be wise to go home now. Not until the killer was caught. Anyone smart enough to evade the US Marshals wouldn't have any trouble finding a small-town chef's address and showing up at her door. She didn't want to be there when he arrived.

She thanked Knox before turning away with Nash. He set a palm against the small of her back, steering her in the direction they'd come, and the moment was so thick with déjà vu, her mind could barely process it.

Lana and her family had arrived in Great Falls her senior year of high school, and she'd gotten to know several of the Winchesters through a shared love of sports. Great Falls High School frequently played and scrimmaged against West Liberty, and the teens in both towns formed bipartisan friend groups. The Winchesters had been part of hers.

It was after she'd graduated that she'd first set eyes on Nash. He'd gone to the military before she'd ever settled in their neck of the woods. So when Knox, Derek and Cruz walked into the pub where she waited tables, with Nash in tow, she'd taken an immediate interest in this new, unfamiliar Winchester. As it turned out, he was four years older than Lana, with hopes of joining the Marshals Service in Louisville, but she'd fallen head over heels for him anyway.

The force of attraction between her and Nash had been more powerful than anything she'd ever known. The pull had felt like destiny to her eighteen-year-old heart. And the moments they'd shared together, until his offer with the Marshals came through, had been the best of Lana's life. Four years of spring break and summer flings when she came home from college. And stolen moments over holiday breaks when they were both in town. Nash had been discharged during her junior year, and she'd moved in with him following college graduation. He'd been her everything. She'd thought he was her future.

The fallout that occurred in his wake had been unequivocal.

She stumbled over the slat of wood she'd hit him with and fell clumsily back to the moment at hand. "I am sorry for hurting you earlier."

"You didn't hurt me," he said, but she heard the wince in his words when he spoke.

They crossed the sidewalk and street behind the still-gawking crowd, moving swiftly toward a black SUV with tinted windows and government plates. Then he stuffed her unceremoniously inside. Her door had barely closed before his popped open. The dome light didn't illuminate either time.

Nash's body was stiff, his jaw locked and eyes hard. Clearly, he wasn't glad to see her, and the additional pain she'd caused was icing on the awful cake of her night.

Beyond the glass, red and blue carousels of light drifted over onlookers and emergency responders, bathing everything in an eerie and ominous glow. The coroner's van lingered, parked beside an ambulance, and she wondered how long Tim would have to lie there, on display for the morbidly curious, a mangled version of his kind and gentle self.

"What were you doing here at this hour?" Nash asked, jamming his key into the ignition and twisting with unnecessary roughness. "Why were you with the victim when he fell? How do you know him? Who was he?"

"I wasn't with him. I was with my plants," she barked back, suddenly angry at Nash's lack of compassion. "I work here, and Tim was my manager. I went up to the rooftop to water my garden. He didn't know I was up there. I saw the car with Pennsylvania plates arrive. Then I heard Tim arguing with someone downstairs. I planned to wait until they'd finished before sneaking away, but they came to the roof, so I hid."

The memory of Tim's wild eyes when she'd stepped into his view came back in a heartbreaking rush. The warning she'd seen there had likely saved her life. And he'd died only moments later, while she'd run like a coward. She hoped he knew the last thing he'd done on earth was noble and that he'd saved her. Whatever he'd done to earn this fugitive's wrath couldn't be bad enough to undo that incredible act of bravery and kindness.

The choking sob that came next was the emotional undoing her body had been waiting for. And she was powerless to stop it.

NASH GLANCED AT the crying woman in his passenger seat, befuddled, dejected and a little ticked off. "Here." He fumbled to access the tissues he kept inside the console, then he passed them her way.

She snatched them from his hands as if he'd offered a starving animal fresh meat.

He wasn't great at reading women, but she seemed to be angry with him, which only confused him more. She'd nearly knocked him into next week with that board. He'd probably have black and blue abs for a month. He was lucky she hadn't connected that thing with his ribs. It hurt to talk as it was, forget breathing deeply enough to say all the things he wanted. Like why the hell was she involved in this murder? And out of all the people in the entire state of Kentucky, why had it been Lana Iona on that damn rooftop?

The quaint downtown area looked more grim and dangerous driving away from the crime scene than it had upon his arrival barely more than an hour before. Funny how one woman's presence skewed everything. Though Lana hardly classified as just any woman, and her presence had always tilted Nash's world.

She straightened, as if she might've heard his thoughts, and balled the tissues in her hands. "I'm okay now," she said. "I want to help, so we can talk when you're ready."

He gave her a careful glance, unsure how to issue words of comfort. *Is there anything I can do?* seemed a ridiculous question, considering she'd just seen a man killed and had barely finished crying. Asking if she was married or dating anyone, because he'd thought of her every day for the past eight years, also seemed inappropriate, or at the very least poorly timed. "Did you get a look at the man who did this?" he asked instead, sticking to the subject at hand.

"Yeah." Lana stared through the window at her side, avoiding Nash's curious gaze. "He was about the same size as Tim, but I don't know how tall Tim was. Taller than me, shorter than you." She pulled a swath of sleek dark hair away from her cheek and tucked it behind her ear. "He was angry when he saw me. I don't know what color his eyes were, but I won't forget his expression, no matter how long I live. There wasn't any remorse for the life he'd just taken, only fury at the fact I'd gotten away."

Nash swore, the sharp curse breaking free without intent. He readjusted his grip on the wheel and gave his rearview mirror a check for possible tails. The pair of cars behind him was distant and unobtrusive, so he returned his eyes to the road ahead. "You could've been killed," he muttered. "I could've gone to that call with Knox and found you on the sidewalk beside the other victim."

"Tim," she corrected. "His name was Timothy Williams, and he was a really nice man."

Nash groaned. "Maybe to you, but if your friend was on Mac Bane's radar, he wasn't as nice as you think. Bane is near the top of a crime chain powerful enough to make a fair share of law-enforcement officers and government officials nervous. His connections are deep and wide. The network's grip is lethal, and when someone oversteps, Bane squeezes. I imagine that's what happened tonight. Your friend messed up, and Bane made sure it wouldn't happen again. He used Tim to send a loud and clear message to anyone else thinking of crossing him."

Lana rubbed a shaky hand over her lips, and Nash did his best not to think of their sweet warmth or the perfect pressure of her kiss. "I don't understand how Tim would've even met a man like the one you're describing."

"Based on the appearance of that restaurant," Nash said, "I'd guess Tim was involved in money laundering, probably in exchange for the cash up front to do some major renovations."

Lana tucked a fingernail between her teeth but didn't argue.

"My team and I have been hunting Bane for over a year," Nash continued. "This guy is trouble, and he's smoke. Collateral damage follows him like a shadow, and that's all we ever find once we get there.

He helps folks get into debt, usually by loan-sharking or through his illegal-gambling operations. Then he lets them pay it back by laundering his money."

"Does Bane kill a lot of people?" she asked.

The fear in her voice gripped Nash's chest, and his arms twitched with the need to reach for her. But he'd given up that right long ago. "I won't let him get anywhere near you," he said. "That's a promise."

Lana nodded, but he wasn't convinced she believed him. He wouldn't blame her if she didn't. Not after the way he'd left things between them before. When she'd been looking for a commitment and he'd been looking to save the world.

The set of bluish headlights he'd been tracking in his rearview mirror turned away after bouncing across the railroad tracks. Leaving only an older model pickup on the dark country road behind them.

And the truck was picking up speed.

Chapter Four

Nash cursed as realization settled. The truck in his rearview mirror wasn't gaining speed because it wanted to pass, it was gunning for them. Apparently, Nash hadn't been the only one keeping watch at the crime scene, and given the government plates on his vehicle, the single advantage of surprise he'd been holding on to was officially gone.

"What?" Lana asked, scanning his face before turning to look over her shoulder.

The truck flashed its high beams, momentarily blinding them.

"Is that truck chasing us?" Lana gasped.

"Yes."

She flopped back against her seat and adjusted her seat belt. "Okay. So, what do we do?"

"Nothing." Nash adjusted his hands on the steering wheel and centered himself. He had significant training and more experience than he liked to recall in situations like these. Car chases and vehicular attacks were criminal foreplay. In his eight years with the Marshals, he'd experienced his share of fugitives who'd tried to outrun him or had sent an underling to try to run him off the road. He'd managed to come out unscathed every time.

That truth should've given him comfort but didn't. The stakes were never this high. Lana hadn't been in the passenger seat.

He tightened his grip on the wheel, determined to arrive safely at the sheriff's department.

The roads outside downtown were dark, curvy and strangely unfamiliar, thanks to the number of years he'd been away. Still, he'd made the trip to the sheriff's department once tonight already, and he knew it wasn't much farther now. Best case scenario, the goon behind him was a warning, not a hit man. Evasive driving was something Nash did well when necessary. Driving while being shot at would be another challenge altogether.

Lana gaped, eyes wide and mouth open. "Nothing? We're being chased by a fugitive I watched murder my friend. We can't do nothing. We'll be next!"

Nash felt his mouth pull into a deep frown. "It's unlikely to be Bane behind us." More probable, this was a distraction, while the fugitive moved on. "He probably sent a lackey to redirect my focus while he pulls up roots again." Which would mean Nash was moving on again in the morning, and for the first time in a long time he wasn't sure he was ready.

He dared a glance at Lana as the engine of the truck behind them growled more aggressively, launching closer before easing back and repeating the process meant to intimidate.

"Who cares?" she asked, expression wild with disbelief. "This guy's going to run us off the road. You need to do something." Her narrow frame trembled, and her rich brown eyes flashed with anger. The long dark hair he'd once had the honor of running his fingers through now clung to sweaty, tear-stained cheeks, and his heart wrenched further.

"I know what I'm doing," he said, but the words came too deep and gravelly for any sort of assurance. "You have to trust me."

Lana jerked her gaze from his and pressed her hands to the dashboard. "He's going to ram us."

"He's not going to—" The image in his rearview mirror blurred as the truck smacked the SUV's bumper.

The SUV rocked and the tires squealed as they wove across the yellow lines and back, the pickup tight on their tail.

Lana screamed, then glared.

Nash checked his speed, his surroundings and his passenger, then reevaluated his plan to stay the course until reaching their destination.

Lana's chest rose and fell in short, shallow bursts.

"We're going to be okay," he said. "Try to breathe."

"Are you telling me to calm down?" She swiveled to fix narrowed eyes on him. "We're being attacked. Nothing about this is okay."

He returned her heated stare. "You are fine, and we are going to be fine," he assured her. "This isn't my first car chase, and passing out over there isn't going to help anyone."

"We aren't being chased," Lana snapped. "We're being ambushed."

As if on cue, the pickup began flashing its lights and honking in long blasts.

Lana faced forward and checked her seat belt.

The SUV shook with another sharp impact.

Nash guided the vehicle through the hit, thankful for a complete lack of traffic on the dark and winding road. Then he reexamined his surroundings.

A set of double yellow lines flashed and winked in the moonlight before them.

Ahead, signs warned travelers of an upcoming curve followed by a hidden road on their right.

Nash pressed the accelerator.

"What are you doing?" Lana asked, hands on the dashboard again. "There's a big curve coming."

Behind them, the truck raged again.

"Hold on," he told Lana.

"You need to slow down," she returned.

Nash pressed the brake and pulled the wheel, causing the truck to clip their rear fender, as they continued on.

The truck's trajectory changed upon impact, sending it across the double yellow lines. The SUV spun across the hidden side road with a squeal of tires and brakes. The pickup careered along a grassy incline on the opposite side of the road.

The SUV rocked to a bone-jarring halt in the adjacent field.

Lana swore.

Nash's headlights bore into the side of the pickup.

He looked to Lana, who returned his stunned but steady gaze. "Stay here," he said, unfastening his seat belt. "Dial 9-1-1 while I check on the other driver. If anything goes wrong, slide behind the wheel and drive to the police station. Don't stop until you get there."

Nash climbed out and closed his door quietly, then freed his sidearm as he approached the stalled truck.

The world was silent around him, save for the call of night birds, bullfrogs and crickets. And the accompanying purr of two idling engines.

A thick silhouette was visible behind the pickup's wheel. A man, based on the general size and shape.

Nash raised his gun with a secure grip as he stepped carefully around the rear of the truck. "US Marshal," he announced. "Open the door slowly and get out with your hands up."

The pickup's brake lights flashed, and its tires spun hard, kicking up hunks of earth and grass before finding traction and launching the vehicle back onto the road.

Nash took aim, briefly considering a shot at the pickup's tires, but a lack of light made any kind of accuracy impossible. Instead, he ran for the SUV, hoping Lana had had the presence of mind to call for help as he'd instructed.

The driver's side door swung open as he drew near.

"Get in!" she called. "Let's go."

Nash buckled up and shifted into Drive, taking a careful look at her before easing onto the road. Trauma was tough on everyone, especially civilians. He wouldn't be surprised if Lana was in shock after all she'd been through tonight. "You okay?" he asked gently, prepared to provide comfort as needed.

"Emergency responders are on the way," she said. "I called, but it doesn't look like we need them now, so let's just get to the sheriff's department. We probably can't catch him now, and I don't want to try."

Nash nodded, understanding her need for security. Her safety was his top priority now as well. "It's fine," he said. "I got a good look at the truck. I can provide a description for local authorities to put out a bulletin. Maybe something will turn up."

Lana handed him a wrinkled receipt with pen marks. "If your description isn't enough, I got the license plate number."

THE GREAT FALLS Sheriff's Department was a sprawling single-story building with nice landscaping and a small visitors' lot out front. It was one of the few places in town Lana had never visited, a fact she'd always assumed would stay that way.

Nash parked near a row of cruisers. "Ready?" he

asked, staring briefly through the dark interior before climbing out and closing the door.

Not even close.

She pulled in a long, steadying breath and emotionally separated from the stress, the way she had when Nash left her to check on the truck's driver. It was a survival strategy she used at work, when the rush was on and she was sure she couldn't keep up. She'd taught herself to take a deep breath and step back. Break down the necessary procedures. Ignore things she couldn't control and focus on what she could. Then attack the tasks one at a time. Doing this, she'd discovered she could accomplish almost anything.

Busy kitchens and brutal killers were vastly different problems, but the strategies for staying calm seemed to remain the same.

Nash offered his hand when she opened her door, and she reluctantly set her shaky palm on his steady one. His fingers curled over hers, momentarily stealing her thoughts. "It's okay," he said. "I've got you."

She nodded woodenly, then allowed him to lead her into the building.

Several minutes later, they were escorted to a formal conference room with an oval table and numerous rolling chairs. The Great Falls Sheriff's Department seal centered one wall. A table with a coffee maker and stacks of disposable cups stood beneath, sugar packets and creamers on the side. A watercooler and a rolling whiteboard like the ones in crime dramas bookended the open door. The board had markers and erasers at the ready.

Lana took a seat, unsure how long her wobbly legs would hold her. Feigning cool and competent only lasted so long after the adrenaline rush was over.

"Water?" Nash asked.

Lana nodded. "Yes, please."

He returned with two cups and passed one to her before taking a seat. "How are you feeling?"

"Shaken." She took a deep drink of the cold liquid and let the sounds of a bustling department anchor her. "Confused. Mad. Scared," she added. "I know you've told me all this already, but can you go over it again? What is happening?"

"Of course." Nash started from the beginning, slowly delivering the details about Mac Bane, a fugitive on the lam with numerous warrants, based on a lengthy list of serious crimes, most centered around money. "The recent renovation of your restaurant, combined with your manager's murder, suggests Timothy Williams got involved with Bane, likely by borrowing money in exchange for laundering services. Clearly, the relationship went south."

Lana's mouth dried, despite the cup of water she'd just consumed. "I heard Tim apologizing to the other man. He said something was no big deal, or it wasn't meant to be a big deal, something like that. He didn't give details."

Nash nodded. "Did you notice anything different about your boss in the last few days or weeks?"

"Not until today," she said. "He was distracted all afternoon and barely left his office."

Heavy footfalls echoed through the hallway outside the door, accompanied by the low murmur of multiple male voices. A moment later, Knox appeared.

Lana smiled instinctually at the sight of her friend. A pair of uniformed deputies continued on in the hallway behind him. The painful tension in her shoulders released by a fraction, relieved by the familiar, easy comfort of a friend. Knox would be a welcome buffer between her and Nash as well. She'd been fighting a whole host of unwanted emotions since first laying eyes on him tonight, and learning she'd have to stay at his side now, at least until it was safe for her to return home, which could take days, was more than she could emotionally manage.

"Hey," Knox said, shaking his cousin's hand. "I got back here as soon as I could. I heard the 9-1-1 call on the radio. I'm glad no one was hurt." His gaze flicked to Lana. "How are you holding up?"

Nash passed him the crumpled receipt from his pocket. "She's great. She got the license plate from the truck when it took off."

"Nice." Knox accepted the paper, already smiling warmly at Lana. "Good work." He slid a notepad and pen across the table to her, eyes fixed on the old receipt she'd dug from the bottom of her purse not long ago. "Go ahead and write down whatever you can remember about tonight," Knox said. "I'll be back as soon as I can to talk through your night so far."

Nash turned to Lana as Knox disappeared into the hallway. "He'll run the plate through the system and let us know who the truck is registered to. It could be a good first step toward figuring out the driver's name and therefore who in this town has ties to Bane," Nash said.

"Could be?" she asked. "Wouldn't the driver have been the owner?"

Nash inclined his head slightly, forehead creasing. "It's more likely the truck was stolen, but even then, the location of the vehicle's disappearance and the owner's identity might still be useful."

She considered the information, then gave a stiff nod. "Okay." She moved the pen to the paper and began to write, unsure at first if she could put any of her thoughts into words. Surprisingly, the memories flowed from her mind to her fingertips, and images from the night became ink on the lines. Once she got started, she couldn't seem to stop. And she wrote until multiple pages were full, her frantic fingers barely able to keep up.

Nash watched with open concern and curiosity, catching her eyes each time she paused to consider the right way to express one thing or another.

"You're staring," she whispered, the heat of his gaze too much to ignore.

"Sorry."

His deep, rumbling voice sent a cascade of goose bumps over her skin, and the pen froze on the page as she finished scribing her final thought.

She could only pray Nash would misinterpret her shiver as a side effect to the night's events and not to her traitorous body's conditioned response to him. "I'm fine."

"I hate that this is happening to you," he said. "You shouldn't have been dragged into Bane's vortex. This man is a poison."

Lana forced a brave face, tipping her lips into a small, joyless smile. "Well, here I am. I wish I wasn't on your fugitive's radar, but since things had to be this way, I'm glad you're here."

Nash's jaw clenched, and his Adam's apple bobbed. Their gazes locked while she waited for his response. "Do you need to call anyone?" he asked. "Let them know you won't be home?"

"No." Her heart broke a little with the fact, though the truth had never bothered her before. "My parents retired to Montana a couple of years ago. It's just me now."

"No husband? Children? Boyfriend?"

Lana shook her head.

Something she couldn't quite name flashed in Nash's eyes. A moment later, he nodded, body relaxing by a fraction. "You became a chef at the town's best restaurant." There wasn't any sense of shock to the words, but there was abundant, evident pride.

"And you really became a Marshal," she said, her nose and forehead wrinkling. "Who chases dangerous criminals."

His cheek twitched, as if he might be fighting a smile. "Yes, ma'am."

"Do you like it?" she asked, ignoring the ache of loss in her chest. He had left her for the job, after all. The least he could do was like it.

She couldn't help wondering if he'd ever regretted the decision to abandon what they'd built together. Had he thought of her, even once, after going off to chase his dreams?

"Yeah," he said. "Most of the time."

She bobbed her head in response. "Good." At least he hadn't broken her heart for nothing. All she'd ever wanted was for him to be happy, so she supposed at least there was that.

Nash lifted a hand carefully in her direction, easing it against her cheek when she didn't protest.

Lana closed her eyes and absorbed his gentle heat and offered strength.

"I will protect you," he vowed. "I'm going to get Bane, and I'm going to keep you safe while I do it."

She opened her eyes, and the intensity of his gaze tingled the back of her neck and curled her toes inside her sneakers.

The man before her wasn't the same man she'd fallen in love with. He wasn't wide-eyed and ready to brawl. He was steady, seasoned and calm. The version of Nash she'd known wouldn't have been able to sit still when there was so much to be done. He'd have been running wild, barking orders and oozing unmanaged testosterone. This Nash embodied the calm confidence she needed to feel safe, and every fiber of her longed to thank him.

"Okay," she said, holding his gaze as his hand fell away from her cheek. "I'm going to trust you. And you're going to make sure I survive this."

"Deal."

"Deal," she echoed. And despite the horrors of the night, her lips curved into a gentle smile.

If she had to be on the run from a murderous fugitive, doing it with Nash seemed like a worthy consolation prize.

Chapter Five

"All right," Knox said, bursting back into the room, paperwork in hand.

Lana sucked in a deep breath and yanked her gaze from Nash's lips.

He cleared his throat, then spun to face his cousin. "What do you have?"

Knox's brow puckered briefly, clearly not missing the atmosphere in the room.

Lana took the moment to evaluate her emotional stability. A friend had died tonight. She'd been in a car chase and was probably being hunted by a killer. Why was she consumed with thoughts of Nash's hands and mouth?

What was wrong with her?

Shock? Maybe she was in shock.

Lana looked away, cheeks hot and heavy with embarrassment. Nash was in Great Falls to do a job. He'd come back for work, the same way he'd left her for work. His life had never been, and would never be, about her. And that was something she needed to make peace with.

Knox took a seat at the head of the table and passed the papers to Nash. "The plates on the truck that chased you belong to a man in the next county, Logan Miller. Local officers paid him a visit, but he didn't even know the pickup was gone. He was asleep when they arrived. He works a swing shift at the local steel mill and parked on the street when he got home. Says he ate, showered, watched the game and went to bed. He didn't check on the truck after he went inside. So the pickup could've been taken up to twelve hours ago by anyone with some basic carjacking skills."

Nash released a blustery breath, stretching his long legs out before him. "I'm never lucky enough to get a criminal who drives his own vehicle to a crime scene. Why is that?"

Knox smiled. "I don't know. From where I'm standing, you look like the luckiest Marshal alive. Your fugitive found his way to Winchester Country. I'd say he's the unlucky one now."

"Winchester Country," Nash said, a slow smile forming. "I forgot how much I liked the sound of that."

Lana crossed her arms over her, warmed by the men's exchange, chilled by the complicated collision of past and present before her. "When will you be able to confirm Tim's killer is the guy you're looking for?" she asked, turning her eyes to Nash, then Knox. "Were there any eyewitnesses other than me?"

"You're enough," Nash said, sliding his cell phone in her direction. The words seemed to have a double meaning, but Lana pushed the idea aside. "Everything about the timing, location and restaurant's recent makeover tell me it was Bane. The Pennsylvania plates add to my assurance, but let's make it official." He selected a photo from the phone's gallery and enlarged the figure in the image. "Is this the man you saw?"

Lana only needed a moment to confirm. "Yes."

The killer's angry expression was burned into her mind. The photo before her was distant and somewhat grainy, a surveillance image of some kind. And the subject was smiling. But it was undoubtedly the same man she'd seen on the restaurant's roof.

Nash's steely gaze raked over her as he pulled the phone away, probably seeing all the things she wanted to hide. He turned the phone to Knox. "Mac Bane."

"Confirmed," Knox said, glancing at the phone before moving on. "We performed a thorough check of the roof. Lana's name badge wasn't there, and her image is on the restaurant's website. I'd hoped the darkness might've obscured Bane's ability to get a clear view of her tonight, but even so, it'll only take a few clicks to find a clearly labeled photo online."

Nash turned his attention back to her. "I'll keep Lana with me until further notice."

"Sounds good. Let me know if you need anything," Knox said.

Lana's stomach fluttered and her heart pounded. The time frame he'd given was extremely ambiguous. *Until further notice* could mean days. Maybe longer. And she was supposed to spend all that time shacked up with Nash Winchester, the one and only love of her life, while pretending she'd simply stopped caring at some point? And her heart hadn't actually stood up and shaved its legs at the sight of him?

She was definitely the one with the bad luck tonight.

NASH REFILLED HIS disposable cup from the fresh pot of coffee on the table. His cousin's shift had ended hours ago, but he'd stayed by Nash's side, accessing records and establishing timelines for the night's events until nearly dawn.

Lana had curled her lean body in the leather office chair and rested her head on a pillow Knox had also supplied. She'd slept fitfully, but she'd slept, and that was something. Especially considering what she'd been through. Bane knew her name, had seen her face and would likely have her address soon as well. Not easy stuff for anyone to deal with, especially a civilian.

He'd stolen glances at her through the night, each time she'd whimpered or twitched, trying to reconcile her with the woman who'd permanently altered his world. She'd enchanted him the day they'd met, with her casual beauty and devil-may-care ways. She'd been too young and too sweet. He'd been world-weary and jaded, but he'd craved the attention of her wide brown eyes and the caress of her soft pink lips for years. Utterly spelled by her.

He'd almost forgotten how powerful that spell could be.

Now she was older and less fragile but impossibly more beautiful. Her narrow, athletic frame had rounded in all the most feminine places, and her formerly mischievous eyes were an intriguing mix of kindness and determination. Though he sat close enough to touch her, the distance was insurmountable. And he was to blame for the gap.

He never should've let her believe he cared more about becoming a Marshal than her husband.

Nash forced his attention back to the work at hand and winced as his bruised abs gave protest.

The courage and sheer will it must've taken for Lana to stop running and brace herself to attack a man she believed was a killer sent a heavy mix of pride and despair through Nash's veins. He was six inches taller and at least sixty pounds heavier. Yet, she'd fought rather than giving him the chance to catch her. It was a calculated but wise risk, because eventually, his longer, stronger legs would've eaten up the distance she'd gained. And if he'd been a killer... Nash winced again. The possibility that things could've ended much differently tonight hurt far more than his discolored abs.

Maybe now she'd be less irritated at him for all the hours of self-defense lessons he'd begged her to endure. All the horror stories of other women taken, abducted or never heard from again.

In hindsight, he'd probably been a bit of a bummer in their early years, still shaken and tense from his time in the military, trying to find his place in the world as a civilian. He'd joined the army after high school. He'd only ever been a kid or a soldier. The adjustment following his return to Great Falls had been slow. Chasing a position with the US Marshals had given him a goal and purpose, provided hope and kept him focused on things he could control.

Across the room, Knox finished scrawling notes on the whiteboard, then returned his dry-erase marker to the grooved tray with a satisfied look. "What do you think?" he asked. "Good?"

"Yeah," Nash answered on instinct, watching without seeing what his cousin had added to their collection of notes.

"How's everything else going?" Knox asked, gaze sliding to Lana. "Did I sense a possible reunion in sight?"

"No." Nash shook his head in warning. He'd asked his cousins to keep an eye on Lana when he left for the Marshal service, and they'd clearly done an exceptional job until tonight. Thankfully, they'd all been too stupid to fall in love with her in Nash's absence.

Knox lifted a palm, stepping figuratively away from the touchy subject that was Lana Iona. He poured a cup of coffee, then leaned against the wall beside the small stand. "Any word from your team?"

"Yeah." Nash rubbed his tired eyes and willed the coffee to kick in. "They were moved to a high-priority case while I came here for reconnaissance. So their arrival in Great Falls has been delayed."

"How long?"

Nash struggled through a yawn. "I don't know. At the time they were reassigned, I still had plans to spend a few days making exploratory small talk with business owners, reviewing documentation from the chamber of commerce and creating a list of businesses potentially touched by Bane before I needed them. I thought I'd have time to lurk around a little and see if I could get eyes on my fugitive, or at least identify the goons in his charge. I wanted to conduct interviews and determine where he's staying before calling in backup. I shouldn't have needed my team for a week, and now I don't have one." He gulped the rest of his coffee, hating the way things were going and his inability to change any of it.

"Hold up," Knox said, expression hard. "You don't have one what? A team?"

Nash frowned. "Yeah." Hadn't his cousin been listening?

Knox set his coffee aside with a low, humorless

chuckle and returned to the whiteboard. He pulled a marker from the tray and made a list.

Knox, Cruz, Derek, Blaze, Lucas.

When he finished, Knox pointed to the names one by one, beginning with his own. "Deputy sheriff. Private investigator. Private investigator. And if we need them, we also have a homicide detective and an SVU detective." He recapped the pen and set it aside with a smile. "You have the assistance of two local law-enforcement offices, a top-notch PI firm and three of Kentucky's finest law officers. Clearly, you've been away too long, cousin. You're in Winchester Country, and around here, Winchesters get things done."

Nash let Knox's words curl his lips into a grin. He wasn't alone or without a team. And he'd definitely been away too long, he thought.

And his gaze drifted back to Lana.

Chapter Six

Lana woke to the sounds of male voices and the re-lentless glow of light against her closed lids. She squinted and attempted to straighten, causing her curled limbs to splay on the small chair.

The night's events and her surroundings returned with a crash as she caught her balance on the small chair. She wasn't in her bed, and her sullen head-space wasn't the result of a bad dream. Lana had spent the night curled up in a sheriff's department conference room, and her thirty-year-old body felt at least twice her chronological age.

"Morning," Nash said, setting a cup of coffee on the table before her while she squinted and checked the corners of her mouth for drool.

A man in a deputy sheriff's uniform made his exit as she sat taller on her seat.

"Sorry. I didn't mean to fall asleep," she said, stretching her neck and back. "Did you get any rest? What did I miss?"

Nash smiled. "I'll sleep soon," he said. His hair

was damp, and his clothes had been changed, while she was irreparably rumpled. "You didn't miss much, just a little research."

"Did you leave me?" she asked, still eyeballing his refreshed appearance. The words sounded more like an accusation than she'd intended.

Nash rubbed a hand against his unshaven jaw, apparently fighting a smile. He looked down at himself, then back to her. "I used the department's locker room for a shower and change. I had a bag with my things in the SUV."

Lana willed her gaze away from his stubbled cheeks, hating how clearly she could recall the feel of that scruff against her skin and the way her body still warmed at the thought.

She took a few tentative sips of coffee, then sucked down a scalding gulp to clear her head. Obviously, she wasn't fully awake. And she could only imagine what she looked like. Not that it should matter or that Nash was looking. The heat, which was ever-present in his gaze eight years ago, had been replaced with the cool appraisal of a law officer on assignment.

Thankfully, the caffeine began to kick in, reanimating her slowly and bringing much more appropriate thoughts to mind. "What's on the agenda today?"

Knox checked his watch. "Today we find a place to stay. Do you need anything from your home before we head to a safe house?"

Lana nodded, feeling the weight of her reality

once more. It was one thing to spend the night inside a sheriff's conference room, quite another to have to leave. Here, they were safe, but she wasn't sure they would be if they left.

Nash rose and moved to the door. "Then we should get started."

Lana tossed her empty cup in the trash and followed on his heels, hoping there was someplace else as safe as the sheriff's department.

Nash fielded questions about the fugitive from a number of deputies as they passed in the hallway. Each man and woman in uniform gave Lana a long, appraising gaze before moving on.

This wasn't just weird for her, she realized. A murder. A fugitive on the loose. A Marshal in town and on the hunt. None of this was normal for anyone, aside from Nash, and even he hadn't seemed 100 percent confident when the subject of a safe house had come up.

He held the door for her to pass into the sunlight, and they returned to his SUV at an increasingly slow pace. Nash sighed as the rear bumper came into view. The dent was severe, and a taillight was broken. He paced the length of the vehicle, presumably in search of additional damage. "I almost forgot about all this."

Lana's heart rate kicked up, and she worked to swallow. Memories of the car chase rushed back to her, tightening her chest and throat. She scanned the area surrounding the parking lot, searching for signs of anyone who didn't belong. Someone watching. Maybe a suspicious-looking car, waiting for them to leave.

Her shoulders curled forward, and she wound her arms across her churning core.

Nash returned to her, eyes fixed on his phone screen, a deep frown on his face.

"We can't take this ride again. Right?" Lana asked, lifting her chin and squaring her shoulders.

He grunted, looking up to catch her eye. "I'd rather not, but I've been told I'm in Winchester Country, so I'm seeing if I can get us a loaner."

Lana smiled at the familiar phrase. She'd always thought it was sweet when Knox, his brother and his cousins used the term. She'd also assumed it was a commentary on the fact their family was so large. Now, however, the fact the Winchesters were all involved in some aspect of law enforcement gave the term new meaning.

"It's a long shot," Nash said, "but—"

His phone dinged, interrupting his words and drawing his eyes back to the device. His lips twitched in humor. "Well, scratch that. Looks like my cousins are willing to trade me an unmarked ride for this one and breakfast. Got any recommendations?"

She smiled. "Now you're speaking my language. The café at First and Main makes the best breakfast sandwiches in the state. Possibly the world."

Nash tented his brows. "How can I pass on that?"

"You can't."

They took the dented SUV into town, both on high alert, but neither mentioning the tension. Nash parked in a rideshare lot near the main drag toward the highway, then climbed out a little more stiffly than he'd climbed in.

Lana met him at the vehicle's grill, watching as he surveyed the area.

A different town stretched out around them. No more live music and wooden barricades to protect the folks who danced in the streets. No more bobbing bistro lights illuminating the lively scene. At just after eight, there was only good old Kentucky sunshine, couples holding hands, families pushing strollers and locals walking dogs. Nothing but early risers enjoying a beautiful country morning.

Scents from the café pulled Lana forward, fueled by hunger and the terrible cup of black coffee from the conference room.

Inside, the dining area bustled with staff and the chatter of cheery voices. The decor was a bit French-countryside, with whitewashed fixtures, tables and chairs. Faux chandeliers hung overhead. Toile curtains adorned the windows. Baskets of French loaves stood on the service counter.

Lana stopped at the back of the line and inhaled the perfection of it all. The cool air on her skin, the laughter in her ears, the scent of fresh-baked breads cooling on racks. A large chalkboard against the wall displayed the day's menu. It was a detail she hoped to borrow for her own restaurant one day. Though

Lana's café would be earthier, more casual and with heavy homage to her Japanese and Hawaiian heritages. She'd incorporate recipes from both of her grandmothers in the menu and create an easy, island vibe through her use of oceanic colors and decoration. Photos from both locales. Mementos and keepsakes on shelves. She'd been planning her café and its details for a decade.

"Nice place," Nash said, breaking into her reverie. "I don't remember this one being here. Is it new or newly renovated?"

"New," Lana said. "It's one of my favorites."

Nash moved to her side, peering at the menu with knitted brows. "Are you still planning to open a café?"

She turned slowly to look at him. "You remember that?" Owning her own restaurant had been little more than a dream when they'd dated. She was still muddling through culinary school and ruining every recipe she tried giving a little flair. It had taken years to understand the complex science that happened in a kitchen and why her additions often made things worse instead of better.

"I remember everything," Nash said.

Her heart tightened, and her stomach fluttered. Did he remember all the things she did? Picking one hundred sunflowers for a community fundraiser? Camping under the stars? Eating Popsicles and kissing until their mouths were warm again? Whispered promises in the dark?

"Next!"

Lana jumped.

A willowy woman in a pink apron waved them forward. "What can I get you?"

Lana ordered a yogurt parfait and iced chai latte. Nash requested a six-pack of breakfast sandwiches, a half dozen strawberry muffins and three large black coffees. He paid the bill and received a plastic number in return.

Nash leaned against the wall at the end of the counter, watching Lana closely as she joined him. "How are you feeling by light of day?"

"Still shaken," she admitted. "But I'm also a little numb. I know I should be scared, and that comes and goes, but it's also hard to make last night seem real, so I'm trying to process."

He nodded. "Well, I'm here if you want to talk it out. If there's anything you want to know or any way I can make this all more manageable, just say the word. I'm probably the last person you'd want to be exiled with, but I promise to make things as comfortable for you as possible."

A bell dinged, and a pair of white bags appeared on the counter. "Eleven?"

Nash traded his plastic number for the bags.

"Coffees," the woman said, setting the tray of disposable cups in front of Lana.

"Thanks."

Nash held the door for her to pass on their way out. "I mean it," he said. "We're in an unfortunate situation, but it doesn't have to be miserable. I'm going to do my best to make this okay for you."

Lana pursed her lips and nodded. "Thanks. I'll be the perfect witness in your protection."

He frowned but didn't otherwise respond. A friendly reminder Nash Winchester was in Great Falls for one reason only. And as soon as the job was done, she'd be dust in his rearview mirror.

Again.

Chapter Seven

The Winchesters' PI office was housed in a discreet one-story office space downtown and lined in mirrored windows to prevent outsiders from looking in. Lana suspected Derek and Cruz had no problem seeing out, however. She hadn't visited them at work before and wasn't sure what to expect as Nash parked the SUV outside.

She'd known Derek and Cruz for years. They were both her age, cousins and somewhat opposites in appearance, though, like every Winchester she'd met so far, both were brutally handsome. She'd adored them both upon their first meeting, and not much had changed.

Derek met them at the door and waved them inside, checking the street behind them. "Hey." He wore his usual tense expression, Stetson hat and cowboy boots.

Nash frowned. "I wasn't followed." He passed the breakfast bags into his cousin's hand and received a crooked man-hug in return.

"Coffee too?" Derek asked, taking the tray from Lana. "Now, this is what I call a reunion."

Cruz whistled as he sauntered in Lana's direction, tossing his trademark mop of light-colored hair off his forehead. He winked playfully at Nash on his way to embrace her.

Lana's arms latched on to her old friend more tightly than she'd expected, and Cruz lifted her off her feet in response.

"How're you doing, Iona?" he asked, setting her on the ground and looking her over. "You all right?"

"No." The word popped out before she could stop it, and the room stilled for a minute before Derek and Cruz laughed.

She joined them, stunned at her admission and complete inability to pretend in their presence.

Derek passed the coffees to Cruz, then reached for Lana's hand and towed her to a round table beyond the front office. "Food with friends makes everything a little better."

Lana absorbed the office's interior design as she followed. The space was minimalist and decorated in shades of black, white and gray. Beautifully arranged bookshelves with framed photos and artful decor made her certain at least one of the items was a hidden camera.

The baseball glove and bat behind Cruz's desk was probably meant to give the impression he'd just come in from hitting a few balls outside, but the bat was more likely an easily accessed weapon. And given his unparalleled ability to turn any pitch into a home run, no one facing off with Cruz and his bat would be foolish enough to make him swing it.

Both men had framed photos of their wives and children on their desks. One more thing she loved about them both. Derek and Cruz were family men.

Nash waited for Lana to sit before taking the chair beside hers. His expression wavered between approval and confusion. "Y'all see a lot of one another?"

Cruz tossed a muffin in the air and caught it. "Only during softball season."

Lana grinned. "These guys have been losing regularly to my restaurant league for some time now."

"Because there's only two of us," Cruz said, standing instantly taller. "We have to partner up however we can, and everyone's starting families. They cancel to watch their kids play or to coach a small-stuff league of their own. We forfeit due to numbers, but we win when we play."

Lana raised her brows and nodded slowly. He was telling the truth, but it irked him, so she taunted him. "Oh. Okay."

Cruz pointed at her and made a small squawking sound.

Her grin grew.

Derek cracked the lid off one coffee and turned his eyes to Nash. "I'd tell you your girl here has one heck of a swing, but I hear you learned that first-hand last night."

Nash's bland expression was comical.

Lana might've laughed if she didn't feel so awful for hurting him.

Cruz took a seat and bit into his muffin with a wide grin. "See, I wasn't going to bring that up."

"Good," Nash said. "Don't."

Lana extracted her chai latte from the carrier and sipped it gingerly. The easy banter and camaraderie between Winchesters loosened a bit of the tension across her back and shoulders. For a moment, she almost felt like a teen again.

She could still remember the first time she'd told him she loved him, and he'd said he felt it too.

Four years later, he told her he was taking a position with the US Marshals in Louisville, and she could come, if she wanted. But he'd already accepted the job, and her inclusion had felt more like an afterthought than a plan.

Lana wasn't anybody's afterthought. So she'd let him go. And he'd gone.

Chairs scooted over the floor around her, pulling her back to the moment. Her eyes jerked up to meet the puzzled expressions of three looming Winchesters.

"You okay?" Nash asked.

"Yeah." She stretched to her feet to join them, shoving the pinpricks of ancient rejection down deep, where they'd laid dormant for the better part of a decade. Apparently waiting for the most inopportune time to return.

Cruz passed Nash a set of keys, distracting him, while Derek scrutinized her.

Lana mouthed the words *I am fine* to her over-protective friend.

"Derek and I have another meeting this morning," Cruz said. "We'll move the SUV to Derek's place as soon as we've finished with that. He's got a barn big enough to keep it out of sight."

Derek nodded. "Cruz will follow me home, and I'll catch a ride back with him. The truck you're taking is registered under an LLC, owned by a corp that's part of an umbrella company." He circled one hand in front of him. "And so on. It's not getting traced back to us without a whole lot of effort."

Nash passed a set of keys to Cruz.

"I'll move it to one of the lots across the street," Cruz said. "We'll be able to keep an eye on it, without it sitting right out front, until we can get it relocated."

"Also," Derek added, plucking a slip of paper from one of the desks, "this is a good place for you to stay while we look for Bane. I've already packed the truck with a couple bags of necessities. You should be set for several days."

Nash looked at the paper, then at his cousins. Emotion flickered in his deep blue eyes. "Thanks. I need to grab my things from the hatch before we go."

"Yep." Cruz squeezed the key fob, and the SUV's lights flashed outside.

Lana waved her goodbyes, then followed Nash

back into the day. She wasn't in a good situation, but she was surrounded by the best kind of men she could want for teammates.

The fugitive situation seemed to be managed. Now it was her heart she had to worry about.

NASH PULLED HIS borrowed truck onto the driveway of a gray-and-white two-story town house several blocks from downtown. The home had a neatly trimmed front lawn and flowers lining the walkway. A large wooden Welcome sign leaned against the wall beside a red rocking chair and the front door, complete with floral wreath and coordinating mat. The scene couldn't have felt more perfectly homey. Or more absolutely Lana.

"This is it," she said, opening the truck door and moving onto the driveway.

Nash followed her onto the porch, shoving unexpected emotion aside, along with an onslaught of possibilities between them that might have been but never were.

"How many days should I expect to be gone?" she asked, swinging the door open to let them inside.

He scrambled mentally to form a response for the question. "I don't know" was the best he could manage.

The inside of Lana's home was open-concept and equally as charming as the outside. She'd decorated in a rainbow of colors, heavy on the blues, which had always been her favorites. Patterned rugs and shaggy pillows graced the floors and furniture. A thousand framed photos of her family hung on the living room wall, and three giant letters stared back from her kitchen, visible through the unwalled space. *E-A-T.*

He smiled.

"Okay," she said, closing the door with a sigh. "You are clearly too tired to elaborate, and since you're currently the only thing standing between me and some murderous fugitive, I'm not feeling overly confident right now."

Nash cleared his throat, thankful for her wrong assumption and wholly amused by her matter-of-fact tone and word choice. He was certainly tired, but more than anything he was regretting some major life choices. Like ever letting her go. "Sorry," he said, meaning it in more ways than she could imagine. "I guess the coffee hasn't quite kicked in."

"Uh-huh." She buzzed past him and pulled a duffel from the coat closet. "I'll get a week's worth of my things together and hope it's far too much."

The sight of her heading toward a hallway returned Nash to the moment and his senses with a snap. "Hold up." He met her with one held-up hand, then moved down the hall ahead of her, checking the bathroom and bedroom for hidden criminals or signs of forced entry at the windows, before giving himself several mental kicks and returning to her side. "All clear," he said. "What's upstairs?"

"Another bedroom and a home office."

Nash nodded. "You pack. I'll take a look up there."

They passed in the narrow hall, shoulders grazing.

Nash suppressed a groan. *Head in the game, Winchester.*

Lana stood outside her bedroom. "Did you look under the bed?"

He laughed. "Yeah. In the closet and behind the curtains too," he said. His tone was intentionally light and teasing, but the words had been completely true.

He took the steps to the second floor two at a time, forcing distance between him and the emotions he didn't want or have time for. She'd been out of sight, if not out of mind, and distractions were usually plentiful. Typically, he avoided feeling the weight of Lana's loss by going for a run or opening a case file and burying himself in it. But those tactics weren't options now, and Lana wasn't typically attached to his side indefinitely.

Nash needed some new management strategies.

The home's second floor was smaller than the first and quicker to clear. He slipped in and out of the rooms, giving each a thorough check in seconds, before heading back toward the steps. He took his time on the return trip, examining the collection of framed photos she'd arranged in the stairwell. Some of the images were older and familiar, but many were from the years he'd missed. And he'd missed too much. He hadn't been there for her parents' retirement or when she'd graduated from culinary school. He'd missed her beating Cruz, a former teen baseball prodigy, at softball. The weight of those losses felt suddenly unbearable.

"Ready," Lana called up the steps, a mass of bags hung over her shoulder. "I'm trying to pack light, but I'm also trying to think of all the things I need or use in a week's time, and it's a lot. Should I bring more than three books?"

Nash jogged back to her, offering his most understanding and comforting smile. "Bring whatever you'd like. I'll help you get it all to the truck now, and I'll help you bring it all back as soon as we know you're safe."

She bit her lip and nodded. "Okay."

The electricity in her stare immobilized him for several long beats. Was he imagining the chemistry and heat? Projecting his feelings and misinterpreting? He refreshed his most polite smile and shook off the notion she could still want him too. They needed to get moving before Bane or his lackeys made another move against Lana.

She walked past him with a sudden jolt, as if she'd sensed his thoughts or their urgency. "Do you mind if I grab some produce from my kitchen?" she called over her shoulder, as Nash trailed in her wake. "I pick up a basketful at the farmer's market every week, and I just went yesterday before work. I don't want everything to go bad while we're gone."

"Fresh produce sounds a lot better than most of the food I eat at safe houses," he said, knowing it would earn him a scowl.

She frowned on cue. "We aren't eating from boxes and cans just because we're lying low for a while. If there's a grill or working stove, we're going to eat well. Even if there isn't," she said, reaching for a basket on her countertop.

A squeal of tires froze her outstretched arm and sent Nash to the nearest window. The glimpse of a small red pickup, like the one that had chased them last night, wheeled away.

Nash was on the front porch in seconds, but the truck was already rounding the corner.

"Nash?"

He jogged back inside, adrenaline pumping, and cell phone in hand. Local authorities were supposed to be on the lookout for that vehicle, so how had it managed to wind up outside Lana's home? Was the sheriff's department really that small here? "I'm here," he said, dialing as he moved.

Lana stood motionless in the kitchen, face ashen, and bags at her feet.

"Lana?" He closed the distance between them in three long strides, then tracked her frozen gaze to the butcher block before her. A large knife pinned a message to a cutting board.

Keep your mouth shut.

Chapter Eight

Lana's limbs tingled, and her core ached. She was somehow both frozen and shaking. Nash's voice echoed through her ringing ears. It took a long moment for her to drag her attention away from the meat cleaver pinning a threat to her cutting board. She'd paid a fortune for that knife and butcher block. Had saved up for both, and now the cleaver that cut as easily through bones as butter pierced a note left for her by a killer.

Someone who wished her dead had been in her home. Touched her things. Violated her space. Chills rolled over her skin like buckets of spilled ice water.

"Lana," Nash repeated, his voice deeper and nearer. His large, gentle hands landed on her shoulders, turning her to face him. "Look at me."

She wobbled under his direction, pivoting on wooden legs until his blurry form came into view. Then the silent, unbidden tears began to fall.

"Hey," he whispered, widening his stance and tipping forward until his eyes were at her level. "You're okay. He's gone, and I'm here. I've got you."

She nodded fiercely, absorbing the words and willing them to be true.

"Here." Nash opened his arms, and she stepped into his waiting embrace.

She pressed her cheek against the solid warmth of his chest, then rested her trembling hands there as well.

He wrapped her in his strong arms, aligning their bodies until her heart rate slowed to match his, pounding evenly beneath her ear. "You're okay," he repeated. "We'll call Knox and let his guys handle this. Meanwhile, we should go."

He pressed his palms, fingers splayed, against her back, supporting her as she worked to still her shaking limbs. Something about the embrace felt suddenly foreign and unsure.

Lana stepped back, wrapping her arms around herself instead.

Nash Winchester wasn't her boyfriend. He wasn't her anything. He was a protector assigned to a witness, nothing more. She needed to get that straight, and fast, because they were about to be in continuous close quarters for an indefinite amount of time, and so far, she was losing it.

"You okay?" Nash asked, hands lifting uselessly at his sides.

"Yeah." Her gaze bounced back to the cleaver,

and adrenaline punched through her system. "We should go."

Nash swung her bags over his shoulder before she could protest, then he snapped multiple photos of the cleaver and ominous note. He tapped his screen for several seconds, presumably sending the images to Knox so he could take over from here. "I'm sorry if I overstepped just now," he said, tucking the phone into his pocket with a charming smile. "I don't usually hug witnesses."

"It's fine," she said, heart breaking anew. Whatever Nash was to her, she was just another in a long line of endangered people to him. A job to be done. Nothing more.

Nash held her gaze for several beats before motioning her to the front door. "Let's swap this truck for another, then check out the safe house Derek and Cruz gave us. It has a Great Falls address, which means we'll be close enough to get back downtown or to the sheriff's department quickly if needed. We'll be far enough away to stay off Bane's radar while we rest and make a plan."

Lana forced her shoulders back and released a long, shuddered sigh. "Great."

He held the door for her to pass onto the porch and waited silently while she locked up behind them.

She stiffened when he set his palm against the small of her back, and he removed his hand immediately.

It was going to be a long few days.

She turned to face him before opening the truck's passenger door, a new thought shooting to the forefront of her cluttered mind. "When Knox comes to collect the threat," she said, flicking her gaze toward her home, then back. "Will he take the knife and cutting board too? Not just the note?"

Nash nodded.

"I don't want either to be here when I come home," she said.

"It's all evidence now," Nash assured. "Deputies will dust for prints and look for anything I missed. Knox will make sure they clean up after themselves before they leave."

"As long as they take the cleaver and board, I don't care about the rest," she said, then climbed into the cab. "I'm going to get new ones when this is over. Then I'll probably move."

Nash gave a soft snort as she reached for her seat belt. "I'll do my best to make it like none of this ever happened."

He closed the door, and her traitorous heart gave a forlorn thud.

NASH PUNCHED THE address to the safe house into his phone and set the device in the cup holder before pulling away from the curb outside his cousin's PI office. It'd taken a while, but they'd managed to find him another pickup truck to replace the one that had been seen outside Lana's house.

He bit his tongue against the urge to build a case for Lana moving to Louisville with him. If not with him, then near him, for her safety, when this was over. After seeing the threat left in her kitchen, Nash doubted he'd ever feel she was truly safe again, even when Bane was finally behind bars. If one killer could come into her life so easily, he reasoned, then so could another. And what if Nash wasn't around to protect her next time? The answer tightened like a fist in his gut.

She would love Louisville. Two universities, continual activities and a booming restaurant scene. He just had to find the right way to make the suggestion. His town also had all the things she loved about small towns, like plenty of parks, community events and a solid library system. Opportunities to run a much larger kitchen in a much higher-rated restaurant than the Carriage House were abundant. And when she was ready, there would be a greater number of available lease spaces for her future café.

He stole a glance at her unnaturally pale face and rerouted his thoughts. Nash had a killer to catch, and that was the only thing he should be thinking about until the job was done.

He pressed the gas pedal with a little more purpose, suddenly in a hurry to arrive at their destination and get Lana out of sight. He still owed her an apology for the way things had ended between them, but he supposed that conversation had to wait too. He could only hope, when the time was right to broach the subject, that she'd give him the chance to make things right. He couldn't rewind time or erase the pain he'd caused, but he could at least let her know how much he'd regretted the decision each day since, and that she wasn't the only one he'd hurt by walking away.

Nash checked his rearview and side mirrors on rotation as he wound his way through the outskirts of town. He added ten minutes to the trip, avoiding a direct path to the destination, so he could be certain he wasn't tailed.

His muscles and his breath stalled on the final turn, when a large white truck came into view outside the safe house. He reached for his phone, prepared to alert Knox and make a beeline for the highway, taking Lana anywhere but here.

Apparently Nash had been unnecessarily concerned about a tail when trouble was already parked and waiting for them.

"Is this the place?" Lana asked, likely noting their small decrease in speed or Nash's sudden need for his cell phone.

"Yeah. Have you ever seen that truck before?" he asked, hoping his voice sounded more calm to her ears than it did to his.

"Often," she answered, and his chest tightened impossibly further.

Was Lana being followed before Nash's arrival? Had Bane's men been watching her restaurant before she'd known anything was amiss?

The home's front door burst open before Lana could elaborate.

An older woman with graying hair and outstretched arms bounded from the porch. A man of similar age motored along behind her, a wide smile on his round face. "Nash Winchester," the woman called, "you pull that truck in here and hug me right now!"

Nash blinked and nostalgia hit like a freight train.

Lana laughed. "It's your aunt and uncle's truck."

Nash eased onto the driveway as the older couple buzzed impatiently over the lawn. "I haven't seen them in a while. I barely recognized them." And he hadn't expected to see them here. The couple outside his pickup was familiar, but not the same. They'd aged, put on a few pounds and gotten glasses.

"I see them every Monday," Lana said, climbing down from the cab. "They stop by the restaurant for chicken fried steak, potatoes and gravy. It's their weekly night out."

"Lana!" Aunt Rosa called, already abandoning her position on Nash's side of the vehicle, in favor of pulling Lana into a warm embrace.

Uncle Hank met Nash with a firm handshake. "I hear you've had quite the welcome back."

Nash smiled at the understatement. "It hasn't been what I expected, that's for sure."

His uncle's gaze drifted to Lana, and his lips pulled into a deep frown. "I suppose it hasn't."

Aunt Rosa rounded the truck once more, arms up

again, this time aiming for Nash. "We've heard everything you two have been through, and we came right over to make sure this place was aired out and set up for two. There's food in the fridge, fresh sheets on the beds and a stack of towels in the linen closet. We left a bag with puzzles, cards and board games in case the power goes out. That happens sometimes here, and the forecaster's calling for storms."

She rubbed Nash's back as she hugged him, then squeezed a little tighter before releasing him and planting a kiss on his cheek. "We're sure glad you're back. Wish it wasn't like this, but I'm going to take what I can get. I'll call your mother to let her know I saw you and you're okay. You should call her too." Aunt Rosa leveled him with her signature stare. "Okay?"

"I will," he said, suddenly sixteen all over again. "And thank you."

She patted his back. "Good. Mamas worry," she said. "It's what we're made to do. Love and worry. Now, come on inside. Let me show you around."

Nash looked to his uncle, who smiled and ushered him forward.

The house was small and white with a black roof, door and shutters. Two cement steps led to a square front porch lined with a black iron railing. The mulch beds were neat. The grass was mowed, and a grove of ancient trees provided abundant shade and a measure of privacy from the road and nearest houses.

Lana grinned as she strode forward, arms locked with his still-speaking auntie.

"When'd those two get so close?" Nash asked Uncle Hank, falling into step at his side.

"When you left, I suppose," Uncle Hank said. "Rosa wanted to make sure Lana was okay, and the ladies bonded. Then, when Lana's folks moved to Montana, Rosa stepped in to fill the gap the best she could." He tipped his head and looked more closely at Nash. "We've never really understood what happened between the two of you. Lana doesn't talk about it, and you don't come around."

Nash bobbed his head. "It's complicated."

"Always is," Uncle Hank said. "Whatever it was, she's never stopped feeling like family to the rest of us. So if you need anything while you're here, just reach out. Winchesters look after family." He clapped Nash on the shoulder, then marched up the front steps to the door and swung it open.

Aunt Rosa and Lana were in the kitchen, pouring coffee and admiring a tray of Danishes on the countertop.

Uncle Hank chuckled. "We stopped at the bakery near our place. It's Rosa's favorite. She made the coffee and stocked the freezer with casseroles, but we brought a few groceries too. We know how much Lana likes to cook."

Nash smiled. "Lana packed produce from her kitchen."

She set her mug on the counter, brows high and

clearly eavesdropping. "You're going to thank me for those veggies later."

He lifted both palms in surrender. "I'm sure I will."

Lana smiled as she selected a pastry, gaze traveling over the home's simple but homey interior. "Where'd Cruz and Derek get their hands on this place?" she asked. "I don't think I've ever noticed it before."

"That's because of all the trees," Aunt Rosa said. "We wanted to cut some back, but they insisted the trees are part of the charm."

Uncle Hank traded a look with Nash that said he understood the real benefit of all the trees. "The boys give Rosa keys to all their places," he said. "She lives for these calls. Snaps right into action. She's become one of the team."

Lana smiled at Uncle Hank. "What about you?"

"I'm just the driver," he said, tossing a wink in his wife's direction. "I take my orders from the boss. She even keeps a couple of go-bags packed near our front door in case of emergencies. She learned what to put in them on the YouTube. Now if the boys are in a predicament, she can swoop in with everything they need on a moment's notice."

"Nice," Lana said, looking impressed and heavily approving.

Aunt Rosa blushed. "I try to do a good job is all."

"And you do," Uncle Hank affirmed.

Nash wasn't sure if he should laugh or hug his

uncle, but he suddenly missed this branch of his family more than he'd ever realized.

"Coffee?" Aunt Rosa asked, raising the pot in his direction.

Nash shook his head, a strange mix of emotions battling inside him. "No, thank you."

"A tour, then," she said, returning the pot to the coffee maker, then dusting her palms. "This is the living room and kitchen." She opened her arms to indicate the tidy, square space around them. "Cruz knocked out the wall that used to separate all this. He likes being able to see every corner." She pointed to the window across from the front door. "The back patio overlooks Willow Creek. There's a nice grill and patio set out there. The creek goes on about twelve miles to meet the river."

Lana moved slowly toward the window. "Beautiful."

"It really is," Aunt Rosa agreed. She swung her arm to indicate the hall near the front door. "Two bedrooms and one full bathroom there. And that's about all there is. Basement has extra supplies, if you need them. Canned goods, soaps, napkins, guns and ammo."

Lana turned to face his aunt, eyes wide, then laughed.

Uncle Hank rocked proudly on his heels. "The house is monitored at all points of entry by a service Derek and Cruz pay for. I helped set it up. The truck they gave you probably has a tracking device, in case y'all go missing. That's Derek's thing."

Lana swung her stunned gaze to Nash.

"Not that you'll go missing," Uncle Hank backpedaled. "It's just one more base my boy has covered."

Nash offered an approving nod. "It's good to be back in Winchester Country," he said, casting warm looks at his aunt and uncle. "Thank you both for all of this."

Aunt Rosa kneaded her hands and smiled. "If you need anything at all, just call." She grabbed her purse and her husband, then blew back through the front door on a cloud of well wishes and air kisses.

Uncle Hank pulled the door shut with a firm snick behind them.

Nash rubbed his forehead and laughed. "I forgot what it was like around here."

"Rosa and Hank are amazing," Lana said. "Your whole family is kind of fabulous. And before your fugitive came to town and killed my friend, I would've told you this was the best place on earth to set down roots."

Nash let her words settle in. He thought of all the ways his family had been there for Lana when he should've been. All because he hadn't been prepared for her anger when he told her about his offer from the Marshals. He'd been too young, high-strung and stupid to understand or care where her anger was coming from. Too selfish to see he'd hurt her too, unintentionally, but still. And he'd stormed off instead of staying the course. He'd been too proud and wholly undeserving of her time and her love.

"I'm going to take a shower and lie down," Lana said. "And I'd better call my folks before Rosa does."

Nash opened his mouth to respond, but she'd already walked away.

If living with Lana for the next few days didn't kill him, leaving Great Falls without her when this was over absolutely would.

Chapter Nine

Lana moved swiftly down the hallway toward the bedrooms and bathroom of her new, temporary home. The bathroom came first, and she paused to get acquainted. The long, narrow space wasn't too different from the equivalent room at her place. A sink, mirror and toilet were positioned on one side. A linen closet and tub–shower combo stood opposite. A small window faced her in the open doorway. Golden sunlight dappled the sill and danced between gauzy white curtains, as if this was an ordinary summer day. And somehow the sight of it was nearly her undoing.

She stepped into the room and shut the door, needing a minute to regain internal control. She imagined leaning against the wall and sliding dramatically to the floor, where she could sob and have a thorough pity party in private. But her wooden legs wouldn't bend, so she stood there, staring at the sunlight not even a yard full of giant oaks had been able to blot out.

"Lana?" Nash's voice rose on the other side of the door.

She let her eyes drift closed to steady herself. Somehow, her life had gone off the rails, and only a handful of people had a single clue. The rest of the world was moving merrily forward, as if nothing had happened. As if her friend hadn't been murdered. A killer hadn't been to her home. Her ex wasn't in town, assigned to protect her, and drudging up a whole host of other things she didn't want to think about or deal with. And a job she loved likely no longer existed.

"Lana," he repeated, a statement this time, not a question.

"Yeah?" she croaked, then cringed at the gravelly, unfamiliar sound. Her eyes opened, and her shoulders squared.

"I have your things," he said. "Should I leave them outside the door, or put them in a bedroom?"

She turned and opened the door with a small smile. "I can take them. Thanks."

Nash evaluated her, making no move to deliver the bags from his shoulder. "You know you can talk to me," he said. "I don't always have the right words, but I've been told I'm a good listener. And I've been in situations like this a time or two. I might even be a little helpful, if you let me."

She extended a hand. "Actually, I only need the little bag for now," she said. "The larger one can go in my room."

He stepped back, peering down the short hall toward the pair of open doorways she hadn't looked into. "Have you chosen the one you want?"

"No. It doesn't matter," she said. "I'm sure they're both great."

He passed her the small bag, intentionally catching her fingertips in the exchange. "I know now isn't the time," he said, sending a wave of heat up her arm to her chest, "but when you're ready, I'd like to talk."

Lana pulled her hand and bag free, then stepped back and closed the door. She waited, breathlessly, listening for footfalls to indicate his departure.

When she was sure he'd gone and wouldn't knock again, Lana undressed as if her clothes were on fire. She was suddenly desperate to wash the horrors of the past twenty-four hours away. The steaming shower spray hit with startling pressure, and her aching muscles seemed to sigh in response. The adrenaline she'd barely managed since spotting the cleaver in her butcher block released in a sudden gust of breath and tears. Her limbs trembled, and the little fight she had left seemed to swivel down the drain alongside the suds and shampoo.

She emerged from the sweet-scented bathroom many long minutes later, feeling boneless and exhausted, but ready to face the day. She'd left a voice mail for her parents, who were probably doing something normal like having breakfast on the rear patio or enjoying a morning hike. She promised to call again soon, then dressed quickly and hurried back to Nash.

Her high-waisted yoga pants were comfortable and forgiving. The hem of her soft cotton T-shirt met the pants at her belly button, allowing a narrow sliver of skin to show when she moved just so. Best of all, the cut and materials always kept her cool on a hot summer day.

"Lana?" Nash asked, before he came into view. "How was the shower?"

"Good." A shiver skipped down her spine at the sound of his voice. She'd always loved the naturally deep timbre. She hadn't realized how much she'd missed the sound of her name on his lips. And she knew that was going to be a problem. Her usually sensible heart had no sense at all when it came to Nash Winchester, and eight years of training herself not to want him had gone out the window at first sight of his sensual blue eyes.

Nash leaned around the corner, peeking at her from the kitchen, a look of concern on his handsome brow.

She lifted one hand in a hip-high wave, and his gaze fell to her midriff.

"Feeling better?" he asked.

"A little," she admitted. "I'm exhausted and way too relaxed at the moment to fuss or panic, so I suppose that's an improvement over the tension."

Nash smiled.

She took a moment to appreciate him in bare feet and jeans. He looked calm and casual, as if this was his house, instead of a hideout. She couldn't pull off that kind of cool if she practiced for a year.

And noticing the way his T-shirt clung to the angles and planes of his chest only served to raise her pulse. The lucky material strained against his biceps and vanished into the low-slung waist of his jeans.

"Can I get you anything?" he asked.

Lana pulled her gaze from his body and fixed it on the coffeepot, unable to make eye contact after being caught ogling. "I think I could use a little more caffeine."

"You must be hungry too," he said. "You left your parfait with Derek and Cruz. I meant to grab it from the bag on our way out, but I forgot. I can make you a proper breakfast now if you'd like."

She blinked, unsure if she was impressed or mildly offended. She was the chef, so it reasoned that she should do the cooking. But Nash was temporarily in charge of her well-being, so maybe that included not allowing her to starve. "Okay," she said, curiosity overtaking her. "What are you making?"

Nash's lips quirked, obviously fighting a smile. "French toast?"

"That will go perfectly with coffee," she said.

He filled a mug and delivered it to her hands. "Everything does," he said.

They locked gazes, and suddenly the small table near the rear window seemed much too far away to wait for breakfast. She set the coffee aside and hopped onto the countertop, prepared to observe Nash's new cooking skills and enjoy the magnificent view while she was at it.

He grinned. "Sticking around to get a good look at my techniques? No pressure, huh?"

Lana raised the mug to her lips, while he cracked two eggs into a bowl with a smile.

"I'm no chef," he said. "My form is probably all wrong, but this is Nana's recipe, so I'm confident you'll approve of the results. Nana is very good."

Lana savored the moment and her steamy brew, thankful for a safe house where she could reset her mind. And a barefoot hunk who wanted to cook for her. "I've never met your nana," she said. "Does she still live in Florida?"

"Yeah. You'd like her." He whisked the eggs, then added a pinch of this and that, while Lana let her mind wander. "She and my mom are carbon copies, in personality and looks. If not for the age difference, you'd never be able to tell who was who."

Her mom was a lot like her grandmama too. It begged another question she wasn't sure she wanted an answer to. Was Lana like her mother? She'd be honored if she was.

"Have you called your parents?" Nash asked. "You might want to tell them before they hear about what's going on from anyone else in town, who won't have all the facts."

"I left a voice mail after my shower," she said, setting her empty mug aside. "They're going to have a bunch of questions and want to come here to take me home with them. You might have to talk them down."

Nash removed the pan from the stovetop and

turned off the burners. "I'll do what I can," he said. "It'll seem counterproductive to them that you're staying here, where you know Bane is also. But trust me, if I thought putting you on a plane would keep you safe, we'd have gone straight to the airport last night." He ferried a plate with French toast and a fork to her side, then set a napkin beside it. "He has your name. Knows your place of work and home address. If you go missing from town, it will only be a matter of time before he looks for you at your parents' home or tries to use them as leverage to draw you out."

Lana felt her mouth go dry and her head become light. She hadn't considered any of that as possibilities. Putting her parents, or anyone else, in danger was 100 percent out of the question. That conversation was going to be a tough one.

"Syrup," Nash said, setting a bottle beside her napkin. He returned to the stove, briefly, then back to her with a plate and fork for himself.

The sweet and savory scents rising from the meal made her mouth water. She mentally cataloged the classic ingredients in the air. Butter and eggs. Vanilla and powdered sugar.

He leaned a hip against the counter where she sat, blue eyes searching hers. "Are you going to try it?"

She lifted the fork immediately, anticipating the heavenly taste.

She slipped the golden brown bite between her lips and let the flavors burst on her tongue. She moaned.

Nash's gaze dropped to her mouth. "Good?"

"Very."

He hummed in obvious pleasure, and Lana pressed her thighs together, fighting her body's automatic response to the sound. Nash was too close. He looked and smelled too good. He was barefoot and feeding her. The trimmings of her favorite fantasy were all coming into play.

His ringing phone pulled him reluctantly back, and she inhaled a breath of sanity while he fished the device from his pocket.

Lana devoured the rest of her breakfast while Nash performed a series of distracted grunts and curses. Whatever news was being delivered, it wasn't good.

He disconnected several moments later with clear agitation.

"What happened?" she asked, rising to her feet and carrying the empty plate to the sink.

Nash rubbed his forehead, then rolled and stretched his neck and shoulders. "That was Derek."

Lana tensed, heart seizing before bursting into a sprint. "Is he okay?" she asked. "Is Cruz?"

"They're fine." Nash frowned. "But someone just drove by their office and shot my SUV."

NASH SENT THE update to his team before driving back to the sheriff's department. The amount of paperwork involved in reporting government vehicles with bullet holes was a nightmare, but the warning that had come with the attack was far worse. Bane's men were on the lookout for his ride, and now that the SUV was in no shape to drive, they would be looking for Nash and Lana elsewhere. Someone had seen the other truck at Lana's place, so he was intensely thankful they'd already swapped it out. Derek would have to hide that vehicle for a while too, in case it came under attack as well.

Lana's gaze traveled over her passenger window, then the windshield, then back, obviously and rightfully on high alert as they returned to the sheriff's department. "Do you think whoever shot your SUV knew we weren't in it?" she asked, dark brows furrowed. "Did they want to kill us? Scare us? What if one of those bullets had missed the SUV and hit someone walking to their car in that lot? It just seems awful and crazy."

"It is," Nash said. "My best guess is that this was a warning, like the threat left at your place and the car chase last night. These things are meant to intimidate and send the message that you can be reached anywhere."

"The shooter could've killed two people in broad daylight," she said. "That's more than a warning."

"Bane's pushing back," Nash said. "He's an animal who's been on the run for three years and is probably feeling pushed into a corner. He's clearly got some kind of business going on here, and a US Marshal showed up five minutes after he killed a man. He knows better than to think he can run me out of town, and you're the only one here who can identify and link him to Timothy Williams's murder. Knox and I are going to go over what he's learned about the shooting and any new details about the restaurant crime scene. I'm also interested in what the deputies found at your place. Maybe fingerprints or something else that can be tied back to Bane."

Lana hiked a brow. "So you have a plan."

"I always have a plan. I don't want you to worry."

"Yeah, right," she said. "This guy is right behind us everywhere we go, sometimes literally. That scared the mess out of me."

Nash offered an apologetic look. "It's possible that all these miniattacks are more about his underlings than you or me. Every time he sends people to do his bidding, he proves his dominance to the newer, possibly less obedient or fearful lackeys. Getting others to commit crimes for him reinforces that he's the boss."

Lana released a labored sigh. "Like killing Tim to make a point."

"Yes," Nash said. "He has to set a precedent. Once the ranks stop listening to him, he's no longer the boss. Bane is fairly new here, so it's possible the knife, the chase and the bullets were the work of local rats running his errands while he makes a name for himself. I plan to bust all that up before he has a chance to spread his poison any further than he already has."

"I hate this guy," Lana said. "And his little helpers. What is wrong with people?"

"A lot of things are wrong with a lot of people," Nash said. "I've stopped trying to figure them out."

He pulled into the parking lot at the sheriff's department, then parked and circled the hood to help Lana out.

She didn't pull away when his hand found its way to her back once more. Inside, they followed a deputy to a conference room with a sheet of paper taped to the door. Nash's name was printed neatly across the center in black marker.

The deputy swung the door open for them to enter but remained in the hall. "Consider this your space for as long as you need it," she said. "No one will come or go without permission or appointment."

"Thank you," Nash said, shaking her hand before she took her leave.

The room was smaller than the one where they'd spent the night, but it had all the same trappings. Table, chairs, whiteboard and coffeepot.

Stacks of manila file folders had been arranged on the table.

"Your temporary office came with a lot of paperwork," Lana said, pushing the door shut behind them.

"These are the files I requested on Mac Bane," Nash answered. "It's everything I know, and everything the deputies here need to know, if we have any hope of bringing him in."

Lana shifted her attention from the files to Nash. "These are all about Bane?"

Nash dipped his chin in affirmation, and she fell onto a chair at the table.

She set a hand on the nearest folder. "Can I look?"

"They're technically all confidential," he said. "Anything you read can never be repeated, but honestly, I could use the extra eyes."

Lana wet her lips and watched warily. "Thank you for trusting me."

It was the least he could do, given her circumstance, but also, he did trust her. Always, and with anything. "If Knox thinks we're crossing a line, maybe we can get you sworn in temporarily."

"Sure." Lana laughed, and the sound raised a smile on Nash's lips.

Someone knocked, and the door opened.

Knox appeared. "Good. You're here," he said.

Lana started, then clutched the open folder she'd been reading to her chest.

Nash shook his head, feigning disappointment when he caught her eye. "Smooth."

Knox grimaced as he pulled the door shut behind him. "I've got an update on Lana's place. The butcher block, note and knife were taken to the lab for processing," he said. "It'll be a while longer before we get any feedback on fingerprints, but I'll let you know as soon as I hear anything on that. Meanwhile, a new team is performing a secondary sweep of the premises now. They should be done shortly."

Lana wrinkled her nose, reflecting Nash's thoughts. "What are they sweeping for?"

Knox crossed his arms and rocked back on his heels. "Anything that doesn't belong."

"That's not very specific." Lana set the file aside and mimicked his body language. "What's going on?"

"Nothing yet. We're being thorough." Knox turned to Nash. "How do the files look? Is this everything you were waiting on?"

"We just got here," Nash said. "But it looks like about the right amount. I'll know more in a few hours. Thank whoever got these shipped for me."

Knox nodded. "My guys spoke to some of the other Carriage House employees. No one noticed anything unusual about the vic's behavior in the days leading up to his death. I'm on my way to meet the team at Lana's place, while the lab runs a ballistics report on the casings found near your SUV. Give me a holler if you need anything in the meantime."

"Will do," Nash said.

Knox lingered at the door, gaze slipping from Lana to his cousin once more. "We've got vests for your protection if you want them. Three attacks since last night is more than a little concerning. I hate to think about what could happen next."

Lana blanched, and Nash moved to her side. "Thanks," he told Knox. "It's appreciated."

He let himself out, and Nash released a long breath. There was plenty of work to do, but at least Lana was safe inside the sheriff's headquarters.

"What did that mean?" she asked. "Do I need to wear a bulletproof vest now? Everywhere I go?"

Nash pressed his lips together, hoping things wouldn't come to that. "Not yet." He motioned to the file-covered table before them. "For now, I thought we could use the information in these files to set up a Mac Bane crime board. What do you think?"

Her resulting smile was all the answer he needed.

Chapter Ten

Lana rubbed her eyes and flopped back into her chair. Hours had passed since they'd arrived at the department, and the words on the pages before her had begun to blur.

She bent her legs and pulled her thighs against her chest. The muscles in her back, neck and shoulders moaned in relief from the stretch. She'd read every word in more than half of Bane's files, stumbling slowly over the things she didn't immediately understand and asking for Nash's assistance with acronyms and unfamiliar terminology more often than she'd expected would be necessary. In the end, she was fuzzy on a few details, but the big picture was perfectly clear. Mac Bane was a monster.

He killed without remorse, and his only goal seemed to be power. He reached that objective through the intimidation of people and accumulation of wealth. The latter was most commonly accomplished via money lending and laundering. He had a reputation as a loan shark and was listed in numerous files where men and women had been beaten, or worse, when they became unable to pay.

Nash groaned. "Nothing in these files explains why he's in Great Falls. I'd hoped to find a proverbial smoking gun, but I'm not seeing anything definitive. I'll ask Knox to talk to members of the city council about all the rejuvenation downtown. Maybe a business will stand out as becoming more upgraded than the grants should've made possible."

"Like the Carriage House," Lana said.

"Exactly." Nash tapped a finger to the file in front of him. "Follow the money. Find the fugitive."

"He really seemed to like loan-sharking and money laundering," Lana said. "Small farming communities like ours are notorious for financial struggles. There's definitely opportunity here for someone like Bane. People get desperate when times get hard."

Nash listened, letting her work through the things he probably already understood clearly, while she tested them on her tongue and in her mind.

"The downtown revitalization project would make it easy to hide the laundering," she went on, feeling the pieces snap into place. "So many shops are being renovated at one time, no one would be suspicious of any one place becoming suddenly nicer or busier. We're a new location to Bane with people primed to manipulate. Our crime rate is significantly below the national average. Our sheriff's department covers Great Falls and half the county. They're spread thin, but usually that's not an issue. People are nice here. And trusting. He could've been operating quietly here for months."

"I think you're right," Nash said. "Now we just need to figure out what he's been up to, specifically, and who's involved. That should help us get a handle on why he killed your boss and where we can find Bane now."

"The Carriage House had a huge renovation last year," Lana said. "Does that mean Tim was using the business to launder dirty money? Can we get a list from the town council on which businesses received grants and for how much? Maybe Tim kept receipts from the workers that we can match with the amount provided by the council?"

Nash spun a folder in Lana's direction then slid it across the table to her. "The financials look good. Tim kept clear, well-documented records, and the restaurant was debt-free. It's as if your boss paid cash for everything, renovations included. We've requested details from the town council, so we'll see if he spent what he was given, or more. Either way, it's important to remember records can be fudged. Some of the most corrupt businesses I've seen have had the most meticulous records."

"So either Tim was an incredible, respectable, detailed businessman or a total fraud?" Lana asked, hating that the latter was a possibility. She returned her feet to the floor with a thud and a sigh.

Nash pressed his lips together in confirmation. Now they had to wait.

Lana paged through the file he'd passed her, recognizing some of the line items on photos from the monthly ledger. She straightened. "I might be able to confirm some of these charges and their totals. I'm familiar with our food deliveries, the costs and content. I order and sign for most of them." She'd also given the overall costs for operating a smaller, but similar, business a lot of thought and research since starting plans for her own café.

"What do you think about the numbers you see?" Nash asked. "Initial thoughts? Gut response?"

"They look good," she said, running the tip of her finger down the page in search of something that stood out as inherently wrong or even slightly inflated. "What if the numbers are right? Is it possible Tim paid cash for things and managed the renovations on council grants and the business savings alone?"

"It's definitely uncommon," Nash said, "but he bought the Carriage House outright five years ago at a good price. He didn't own a home, and he leased his car. That could mean he prioritized cash to the restaurant, treating it as an investment, while making payments on personal things. Unfortunately, without him to explain his motivation and thought process, or his relationship with Bane, this is all speculation. Another downside of investigative research. Even the facts only reveal so much."

Lana folded her hands on the file. "I can see why instincts are so important in this job," she said. "Based on what we know, how do you think Tim fits into Bane's world?"

"I don't know," Nash said, stretching his long legs beneath the table and leaning back in his chair. "He isn't my idea of a perfect fit for money laundering, but I've barely begun to look into him. Any chance he needed a large amount of money recently, aside from the restaurant renovations? Sick mother? Extensive medical bills for someone he loves? Recently involved in a lawsuit?"

Lana shook her head. "Not that he ever mentioned. Tim and I weren't friends outside work, but he was a good guy. Not a criminal. Maybe he saw or overheard something he shouldn't have, like I did."

Nash gripped the back of his neck, massaging the muscles there, then along the top of one shoulder.

Lana tried not to admire the flex of his impressive biceps with each squeeze and knead.

"I don't know," he said finally. "What are the odds that he was killed for being in the wrong place at the wrong time, and you showed up, in the wrong place at the wrong time?"

Lana puffed her cheeks. No one had ever asked her to guess the motivations of a murdering fugitive before, but when Nash put it like that, the odds seemed incredibly slim.

"Anything's possible, I suppose," he said.

She sighed, slumping forward, and braced her

forearms on the table. Flimsy memories of Tim's last few words floated at the edge of her mind. Had he said he was sorry? That he hadn't meant to overstep? She couldn't be sure. Her thoughts had been too frantic then and too muddled now.

Curiosity flashed in Nash's eyes. "Can you think of anything else he said?"

"Not really," Lana said. "That night's become so fuzzy and surreal."

"What else can you tell me about Tim?"

She rested her forehead on waiting hands and mentally replayed dozens of conversations and many more memories. "He loved to play cards. Online. With friends. He was friendly, but not outgoing. He spent a lot of time with a small circle of friends."

"Did he gamble?"

"I don't know," she said, another theory coming to mind. "If he gambled more than a little, it could give a different explanation for why he doesn't own his home or car," she said. "Maybe his credit is bad and he can't get loans." She considered the idea a long moment. Nash was right. Without context, facts only told part of the story.

"Who does he play cards with?" Nash asked, flipping his phone, screen up, on the table.

"I'm not sure. He and his buddy host a guys' night out on most weekends, but I don't know who the other guys are," she admitted.

Nash smiled, and a low vibration of energy seemed

to rise from him. "Gambling is one of Bane's favorite pastimes. Observing, not playing. Where there are gamblers, there are lots of opportunities to loan money. When they keep losing and can't pay him back, he owns them."

Lana felt the thrill of Nash's approval in her core. "So they agree to launder for him," she guessed.

He nodded slowly, eyes crinkling around the edges. "Now we have something to look for. Any ideas where an illegal-gambling operation could run without drawing attention in this town?"

She shook her head. "No."

Nash lifted a pen and made a note on a pad of paper at his side. "Let's pose the same question to my cousins and the deputies. See if they have any ideas. What else can you tell me about the guys' nights?"

Lana frowned, frustration replacing the temporary pride. "Nothing. I never listened once the subject was broached. I wasn't interested, and his plans weren't any of my business," she said.

"What do you know about his hobbies and hangouts?"

She racked her mind for new ideas, forgotten memories, anything that might become a new lead. "I don't know. He was a flirt. Put on a big show to check on customers. He was handsome and charismatic when he wanted to be. People liked him. He dated a lot."

Nash's jaw locked, and he rolled his shoulders,

as if trying to dislodge the tension. "Was he close to anyone in particular that you know? Hooking up with someone regularly who he might've spoken with candidly?"

Lana considered the question a moment. "He sometimes hooks up with Heidi," she said. "Heidi tends bar on the weekends and helps wait on large parties during the week."

Heidi was a flawless server with the memory of an elephant and an unparalleled flirt. She earned more from tips on any given weekend than Lana made in a week's salary.

"Would he have spoken to Heidi if he was in trouble with someone like Bane? Is it possible she knows something that can help us find him?" Nash asked.

"I don't know, but I can ask," Lana said, pulling the cell phone from her purse. She paused before dialing, suddenly unsure. "Do you think she knows what happened?" She wasn't prepared to deliver the news of Tim's death. Asking Heidi personal questions she wouldn't fully understand was going to be tough enough.

Nash moved to stand beside her, resting his backside against the table as she dialed. "I doubt there's anyone who hasn't heard he's gone, but you were the only witness, so we haven't declared the fall a murder."

Lana gaped at him, as the phone began to ring. "What are people supposed to think? He killed himself?"

"Or fell," he said. "We don't want to show our hand by naming Bane a suspect. It's enough he knows I'm in town. If he thinks there's a chance he can stay hidden and wait me out, we want him to think that. Anything is better than setting him on the run again. We want to keep him guessing about how much they know. Also, the sheriff's department is trying not to instill panic in the public."

Lana pressed her phone's speaker and held her breath through the endless tinny rings.

"Hello?" Heidi croaked.

Lana straightened, gaze jumping to Nash. She'd given up on expecting an answer. "Hey, Heidi," she started. "It's me, Lana. I wanted to check in and see how you're holding up after what happened to Tim."

A round of sudden sobs crackled through the speaker. "He's gone," she said. "I saw it on the news, but I can't believe it's true. I keep calling him, thinking he'll pick up and tell me it was an awful misunderstanding, but he doesn't answer." Her words broke off, and wailing began.

"I am so sorry," Lana said. "I know the two of you were…close."

Nash circled a finger.

She inhaled a steadying breath, supposing he meant for her to get to the questions. It was nice to feel useful, like a participant in the process instead of the victim, but she was significantly out of her comfort zone. "I hate that you're going through this," she said, speaking from her gut. "I wish it hadn't happened, and I don't mean to push when you're hurting, but do you have any idea what could've led up to this for him?"

Heidi's wails quieted. "What do you mean? The news said he fell. It was a fluke. An accident."

Lana snapped her gaze to Nash's. "I heard him on the phone before I left last night. He seemed upset."

Nash tapped his phone screen.

"Are you suggesting he jumped?" Heidi squeaked. "Is that what you're saying?"

"No, of course not. I'm not suggesting anything. I'm wondering if you knew what was going on with him lately. He was agitated all day, and then this."

Heidi made a guttural sound and began to sob once more, struggling for breath between screeches.

Lana turned desperate eyes to Nash, with no idea what she was supposed to say.

He fielded incoming texts.

"He was trying to do better with his life," Heidi said between sniffles. "He was trying to make things right. We were going to run away together and leave this place behind."

Nash turned his eyes to her, brows raised.

Lana spluttered, struggling to form another question around the shock. "Really?"

"Yes, really. We were in love. It just took him a while to realize it. I knew right away," she said, a small laugh breaking through the tears. "But he kept his feelings under wraps until a week or two ago. I've been telling him from the start that we were meant to be together. He finally knew I was right, and it was the best news of my life."

Lana ran mentally over Heidi's words, trying to put herself in her friend's position. "So he was cautious about your relationship, until a couple of weeks ago when he suddenly changed positions? Any idea what happened in between?"

"No." Heidi said, sounding a little breathless. "I thought he was going to break it off with me again. He'd been so distant, taking Sandy out all the time and spending every evening with Mickey. I thought he was gone, then there he was, asking me to run away with him."

"Who are Mickey and Sandy?" Lana asked.

"Wait a second," Heidi said. "I might have company."

The line was silent for a long beat.

"There's someone at my door," she said. "I'm going to have to go. It's probably Mickey. He'll want to talk, and I could use the company."

"Wait!" Lana tossed the word across the line, but it was too late. Heidi had disconnected.

Lana slunk back in her chair. "Did you hear all that?"

Nash nodded. He tapped his phone screen several times, then turned the device to face her. A mug shot was centered on the screen. "Ever seen this guy?"

Her lips parted as she examined the photo and

the lengthy list of previous arrests listed below. One crime stuck out above the other. Illegal gambling.

She turned her stunned gaze to Nash. "That's Tim's friend Mitchell Edwards."

According to the text beneath the photo, he also answered to Mickey.

Chapter Eleven

It was nearing dinnertime when Nash got things settled at the sheriff's department. He'd spent longer than he'd expected relaying his theory of a possible underground-gambling operation in Great Falls to the sheriff's department, then filling in his team by phone so they'd know what they were walking into when they finally arrived in a day or two. He'd sat through multiple meetings with the county sheriff, deputies assigned to the case and lengthy phone calls with his cousins, whose PI firm had been brought in as consultants and added resources.

Lana was outwardly patient and pleasant through it all, but Nash could see she had things she wanted to say, and he wanted to hear them.

Hopefully, she'd open up over dinner at the safe house when they were in for the night and could talk through the tougher aspects of the last twenty-four hours. Lana was in a miserable situation, and he hated that for her. She was a doer, not a waiter, and despite her calm exterior, he was sure she was ready to scream.

She should be able to do that if she wanted.

He shouldn't have asked her to help with the research today. The goal had been to give her something productive to do so she wouldn't feel helpless or want to explode. The downfall he should've seen coming was that Lana was insightful and highly motivated to get the job done. And doing all she'd done, on top of being removed from her home and losing a friend, was too much to ask of anyone. Lana was a civilian in his care, and he'd caused her more distress when he should've been doing everything he could to make her more comfortable.

He'd even let her call her coworker Heidi and ask about their fallen boss. That had to have been traumatizing. So why, when he should've been ashamed of himself, was he feeling so darn proud that she'd gained information with that conversation?

Lana had given them a new direction for the investigation. Tim had planned to run away, and he'd recently spent a lot of time with Mitchell Edwards, a known criminal, and someone else named Sandy.

Nash caught Lana's eye as she returned from a trip to the ladies' room.

She frowned when he smiled.

"Hungry?" he asked. He'd been starving for hours, so she must be too. The mere mention of a meal caused his stomach to cheer.

Lana stopped in the doorway. "Are you finished here?"

"I am," he said, rising to meet her.

She collected her purse from the small table, then fixed him with a cautious stare. "I think we should drive by Mitchell's place before we go back to the safe house," she said. "I know him. You and everyone else here have spent the day talking about him as if he's a criminal, and maybe he was once, but he's a genuinely nice guy now. He came to the restaurant almost every weekend. He ate wings and talked about the game with the staff. I like him," she said, her voice going soft. "And he was close enough to Tim to know something useful."

Nash followed her back into the hall. "I'm sure a deputy was already dispatched."

"I'd still like to talk to him," she said, peering into Nash's eyes as they made their way through the building. "Mitchell and I were friendly, and we both cared about Tim. I want to know what's going on. Heidi's too wrecked to put three words together, assuming she knows anything at all. Mitchell could be an excellent resource."

Knox appeared around the next corner, talking with another man in uniform. He stilled when Nash and Lana came into view. "You guys headed out?"

"We were thinking of stopping at Mitchell's place," Lana said. "Have you sent anyone to talk to him yet?"

Knox cocked a brow. "Yeah. No one was home." He dragged his gaze to Nash.

He pinched the bridge of his nose, fighting off a

headache that had been brewing all afternoon, and willfully ignored the pangs of hunger. "Lana thinks this guy might talk openly with her about what's going on, given their mutual friendship with last night's victim," he said. "We'll let you know how it goes if he's home. Then we're picking up dinner."

Lana turned a knowing look on him. "I can make something when we get to the safe house. Your aunt brought all that food."

Nash nodded, too exhausted to argue that she'd had a long day too. "That works."

She beamed, and Knox shot him a warning look as they moved on.

The idea of her cooking for him incited an onslaught of similar memories. She used to love cooking for him. It was how she'd first won him over. Her age had been a major red flag when they'd met. She was barely out of high school, and he'd already put in several years as a soldier. She was all goodwill and happy thoughts. He had a career plan that involved hunting killers and criminals. He'd wanted a woman who was tough and maybe a little jaded. Someone he could relate to. Someone more like the women soldiers he'd served with and less like a romance-movie heroine. He'd planned to let her down easy when he arrived for their date, but she'd cooked for him. The entire experience, from the conversation to the meal to the chaste goodbye kiss, had changed his mind and his future. She'd ruined him for every other woman with one meal.

MITCHELL EDWARDS'S NEIGHBORHOOD was of the older, working-class variety, with mature trees and neatly cut lawns. Kids rode bicycles on the sidewalks and played kickball in the street.

Nash parked the truck at the end of the block and took a minute to thoroughly examine the area before climbing out.

Lana followed his lead, then grabbed his hand and nearly dragged him to the small brick bungalow.

Nash dug his heels into the sidewalk at the bottom of the porch steps. "Door's ajar."

"What?" She wrinkled her nose. "How can you know that from here?"

"Look at the shadows," he told her, releasing her hand in case he needed to access his sidearm. He took the lead, moving slowly and setting her behind him as he made his way up the front walk. "Text Knox. Let him know about this," he said, releasing the snap on his holster.

If Bane was inside, Nash could grab him and end this mess today. But if things went south, Lana could get hurt. Asking her to wait in the truck wasn't the answer, and he had severe reservations about turning his back on a home where Bane could be armed and watching them. "Stick close," he said.

She curled her fingers in the back of his shirt, and they climbed the porch steps together.

He toed the door open and scanned the still, dark space. "US Marshal," Nash announced.

Silence gonged in response.

"Mitchell Edwards," Nash tried again, "I have a few questions I'd like to ask you."

Lana clung to him like a second skin, conforming her every movement to his. Her steps were soft and her breaths silent. If her fingertips weren't actively setting his every nerve on fire, he wouldn't have even known she was there.

Slowly, they moved room to room. The space was well-maintained and tidy. A row of shoes lined the wall beside the door. A closed laptop sat on a desk in the living room. Every dish was washed and put away in the kitchen. The second floor revealed more of the same, until they reached his bedroom.

The bed was unmade, dresser drawers stood ajar, their meager contents in disarray. The double doors of a closet yawned open, its contents partially emptied, the remaining items hung askew.

Lana separated from Nash and gaped at the overturned room. "He ran?" she guessed.

"Appears that way." Nash snapped several photos for Knox, disappointed but unsurprised.

The otherwise-tidy Mitchell Edwards had cleared out in a hurry, not bothering to cover the fact he'd run. The haste spoke of fear. And the fear screamed of Mac Bane.

Nash led Lana back down the steps. Local deputies would need to take over from here.

A figure came into view outside the front window, and Nash froze.

He motioned for Lana to stay where she was, then he crept to the door, hand back on his gun.

A woman slipped inside, then screamed when she saw him. She was young and lean, dressed in scrubs and not too happy. "Who are you?" she asked, eyes tight and voice hard. "What are you doing in there? Where's Mickey?"

Nash flashed his badge. "US Marshal. Do you have a minute to answer a few questions?"

She folded her arms and nodded. Her gaze sweeping to Lana, before returning to Nash. "Who's she?"

"I'm a friend of Mitchell's," Lana said.

The woman's eyes narrowed further. "What are you doing here?"

Lana stepped forward. "My name is Lana Iona. I'm a chef at the Carriage House. Mitchell came in to visit with my boss a lot."

The woman seemed to consider the information, then swung her attention back to Nash. "Pam Reynolds. I live across the street. You haven't told me why you're here when Mickey isn't. Does this have something to do with what happened last night?" she asked.

Nash gave a small, stiff dip of his chin in answer, still assessing the woman before him.

"I knew he didn't fall."

"You knew Tim?" Lana asked.

Pam shrugged. "He was with Mickey a lot lately. I didn't hear about what happened to him until I got to work this morning. I tried calling Mickey all day, to see if I could bring him anything when my shift ended, but he didn't answer. I came straight here after work."

"Any idea where Mr. Edwards might be now?" Nash asked.

Pam shook her head, skin paling. "You don't think…"

Nash pressed his lips together. "We don't know. No one has seen him today."

Lana shifted, anxiety rolling off her in waves. "Anything you can tell us about Mitchell and Tim… or Sandy would be very helpful. We want to protect whoever we can."

"Sandy," Pam repeated, expression wrinkling. "Do you think he took her out?"

Lana slid her gaze to Nash, then back. "Maybe," she said. "Do you know her?"

Pam frowned and raised a finger toward a framed photo of Mitchell and another man on the mantel. The men stood on a dock, arms draped over one another's shoulders. "That's Sandy."

Nash retrieved the photo for a closer look.

Behind the men, five large black letters were visible on a boat.

S-A-N-D-Y.

Chapter Twelve

Her mind racing, Lana buckled into the pickup truck beside Nash. According to Pam, Mitchell kept *Sandy* at the marina, so that was the next stop. No question. What was much harder to get her mind around was how Tim and Mitchell had become involved with a murderous fugitive. They were two of the most ordinary men she knew. Most confounding was Mitchell's lengthy list of previous arrests. Clearly she had wildly inaccurate notions of what criminals looked like, and it begged even bigger questions. Was she wrong about anyone else she knew? Was everyone not quite what they seemed?

"What are you thinking?" Nash asked, piloting the truck back through town.

Lana gave the handsome Marshal at her side a long, appraising look. She'd been wrong about him once too. Not the part where she believed he would reach his career goals and become an incredible Marshal but the part where she thought he'd loved her in the same way she'd loved him.

He stole another glance in her direction when she didn't answer. Nash had always been observant, but the years seemed to have honed his natural skills, and she squirmed a little under the scrutiny.

"Everything," she said finally, unable to pinpoint a place to begin. She let her head rest on the seat-back and stretched an arm through the open window, clutching at the warm summer air as it beat against her palm.

It'd been a day like this when she'd first cooked for Nash. She could tell that night that he thought she was too young and naive. He'd experienced things during his time overseas that had altered and hardened him. She'd only experienced high school and the safety of small-town life. The four-year age difference between them had felt more like twenty that night. But Lana had always had a keen awareness about what she did and didn't want. And she'd wanted him.

Her mom always said the way to a man's heart was through his stomach, so Lana had cooked for Nash on the night she believed he'd break things off with her. There had only been on a handful of outings, not even official dates, and her gut said he was preparing to let her down gently. She, on the other hand, had known the moment she'd first set eyes on him that he was the only one for her. She would've done anything to keep him.

Her friends told her sex was the answer, but she sensed sex wasn't anything new or particularly cherished by Nash at the time. With a face and body like his, even eighteen-year-old Lana knew he could get sex anywhere. What he couldn't get just anywhere was a night of good food and general caretaking by someone who was actually invested. So that was what she'd given him.

And he'd stayed for four years.

"You're very quiet," he said, yanking her back to the present. "We can talk through as much of this as you need. I know it's a lot to take in and process. I can help." He smiled, then refocused on the road. "We always had great talks."

The image of their first kiss flashed, unbidden, into her mind. Ignited by the small, crooked smile she loved. The taste of baked apples had lingered on their lips and tongues.

"It's understandable if you're feeling over-whelmed and need a break," he said. "This kind of work isn't for everyone, and I've had you on the case with me since breakfast."

The pleasant memory vanished, leaving her in a truck with the man who had broken her heart, on their way to hunt a criminal. "I'm fine," she lied. She was perpetually afraid and angry, thanks to Mac Bane and his underlings. And she was horrified by the way her hopeful heart still ached for Nash Winchester.

"I know our shared past makes this harder for you," he said, picking at her barely scabbed emotional wounds. "We need to settle this thing between us and start talking openly, Lana."

She stared through her window at the green fields blurring past, unable to meet his eye. He thought their shared past made this harder for her. But not for him.

And she hated that he was right.

"Lana."

She forced her gaze to meet his and measured her words. *"This thing between us,"* she said, borrowing his phrase, "is eight years of loss and hurt. It's my tears and your silence. I'm okay now, and my life was good until last night, but I lost my best friend, my boyfriend and my future all at once when you left, and I've never figured out what to do with that."

His lips parted, but he closed them without interrupting her.

Grateful, she went on. "Your absence hasn't stopped me from succeeding in whatever I put my mind to, but the way you left wasn't right or fair. Now you're back with just as little warning, which is equally jarring, and I'm doing my best to let the past go. My new fear of being shoved off a building, hacked to death with a cleaver or shot in a drive by is a solid distraction most of the time. Also the fact none of this feels real. So maybe we should talk about us at some point. I don't know. Right now, I'm just trying to get through each minute as it comes. And while I appreciate your willingness to talk through our old stuff for my sake, you should be focused on your job right now, not on me. After Bane is caught, we can figure out what we need to discuss, if anything."

Lana turned back to the road and released a small, easy breath. Pride flickered in her chest at the calm and sensible way she'd spoken. She'd acknowledged her feelings without making them the center of their crisis. She'd been honest. And real. And it felt good, when very little had since Tim and Bane had shown up on the roof.

"You are my job," Nash said, hitting his turn signal with unnecessary oomph.

"I'm well aware," she whispered, thankful to spot signs for the marina up ahead.

"That's not how I meant it," he said.

She didn't argue. She didn't have the energy.

Nash guided the truck into a gravel parking lot at the marina and took a spot near the small office building.

Lana climbed out, and Nash met her at her door.

"I'm still struggling to see Tim and Mitchell as criminals," she said, redirecting the conversation from their complicated past. "Both men were completely average and normal in every way. They were known and respected within the community. How did they both get involved with someone like Mac Bane?"

She started walking toward the squat, one-story office space.

Nash followed at her side.

"A lot of nice people make bad choices," he said. "They don't automatically self-identify as a criminal. They usually think that whatever they're doing is only temporary and that they're in control. They think they have a good reason for the behavior, which makes it okay, and they plan to stop as soon as they reach whatever goal they've set in their minds. Unfortunately, people like Bane don't let go so easily." He released a heavy sigh. "Good, smart people do incredibly stupid things all the time."

Lana slid her eyes to meet his. "I know."

They stopped several feet from the office door, both seeming to notice the white vinyl sign at the same time. The rectangular notice was wedged in the front window. Red block letters announced *CLOSED*. A little plastic clock suggested staff would reopen in the morning.

Nash scribbled a message on the back of a business card pulled from his wallet, then tucked it under the door. "Hopefully whoever finds this will call. Otherwise, we'll have to come back," he said. "Do you remember what *Sandy* looked like from the photo?"

"Big white boat with her name on it?" Lana asked.

Nash smiled. His big hand brushed her back as they turned toward the water.

"Maybe she's here and Mitchell's onboard," he suggested. "Two birds. One stone."

If only it would be that easy, Lana thought. She'd also hoped Mitchell would be at his home, but that hadn't worked out either. And his absence sat cold in her gut. She could only hope he hadn't wound up like Tim.

They walked along the narrow, sun-bleached boardwalk, peering at each of the docked boats in search of *Sandy.* A few resembled her from the distance but up close became other vessels altogether.

The dregs of golden sunlight winked on bobbing waves.

Sunset was near. The end of another day in her new, twisted reality.

Lana rubbed the chill from her arms. What had Mitchell and Tim gotten themselves into?

They changed directions at the end of the final dock and headed back to the parking lot. Lana scanned the scattered trucks and boat trailers, mind working overtime once more. "We should look for Mitchell's car," she said. "He drives a white four-door sedan, an older BMW, I think. There's a cling on the back window from last year's fundraising 5K. Maybe he left the car in the lot."

Nash reached for her hand as he picked up speed. "Another good idea. Let's go."

Her chest puffed with pride at his words and hope for another clue, but it only took a few minutes to confirm their mission had failed. No white sedans, BMW or otherwise.

"It's all right," Nash said, unlocking the truck and helping her inside. "This is how it goes some days. One step forward, twelve steps back. Let's go home and eat. Get some sleep and start again tomorrow. I'm running on fumes. You must be too."

LANA WOKE AT five the next morning without prompting. She'd fallen asleep hours earlier than she'd thought possible, given her strange situation, then slept soundly, until her internal clock opened her eyes. Chef life sometimes kept her up late, but it always got her up early.

She lingered in her room until the first signs of dawn passed over her window. She didn't want to wake Nash, but she also needed to clear her head, and that meant cooking. So she padded softly to the kitchen, eager to get started.

The meal she'd prepared the night before had been quick and simple. Seared veggie slices, ears of corn and chicken on the grill. There hadn't been time for a proper marinade, but the results had still been spectacular. The colors and arrangement on the grates, then plates, were exactly the kind of aesthetic she'd use to advertise her café one day. Healthy eating was a lifestyle she wanted to amplify.

She prepped a pot of coffee to brew, sprinkling cinnamon in the grounds before pressing the power button. Then she turned to the fridge.

She had everything she needed for a quiche or frittata but wasn't quite awake enough to tackle a decent crust. "Frittata it is," she said, smiling at her remaining veggies.

Seconds later, she was lost in the work, chopping

Treat Yourself with 2 Free Books!

Suspense

Suspenseful Romance

GET UP TO 4 FREE BOOKS & 2 FREE GIFTS WORTH OVER $20

See Inside For Details

Claim Them While You Can

Claim up to FOUR NEW BOOKS & TWO MYSTERY GIFTS – absolutely FREE!

Dear Reader,

We both know life can be difficult at times. That's why it's important to treat yourself so you can relax and recharge once in a while.

And I'd like to help you do this by sending you this amazing offer of up to FOUR brand new full length FREE BOOKS that WE pay for.

This is everything I have ready to send to you right now:

Try **Harlequin® Romantic Suspense** books featuring heart-racing page-turners with unexpected plot twists and irresistible chemistry that will keep you guessing to the very end.

Try **Harlequin Intrigue® Larger-Print** books featuring action-packed stories that will keep you on the edge of your seat. Solve the crime and deliver justice at all costs.
Or **TRY BOTH!**

All we ask in return is that you answer 4 simple questions on the attached Treat Yourself survey. You'll get **Two Free Books** and **Two Mystery Gifts** from each series you try, *altogether worth over $20*! Who could pass up a deal like that?

Sincerely,

Pam Powers

Harlequin Reader Service

Treat Yourself to Free Books and Free Gifts.

Answer 4 fun questions and get rewarded.

	YES	NO
1. I LOVE reading a good book.	○	○
2. I indulge and "treat" myself often.	○	○
3. I love getting FREE things.	○	○
4. Reading is one of my favorite activities.	○	○

▶ DETACH AND MAIL CARD TODAY! ▼

TREAT YOURSELF • Pick your 2 Free Books...

Yes! Please send me my Free Books from each series I select and Free Mystery Gifts. I understand that I am under no obligation to buy anything, as explained on the back of this card.

Which do you prefer?

❏ Harlequin® Romantic Suspense 240/340 HDL GRCZ
❏ Harlequin Intrigue® Larger-Print 199/399 HDL GRCZ
❏ Try Both 240/340 & 199/399 HDL GRDD

FIRST NAME

LAST NAME

ADDRESS

APT.#

CITY

STATE/PROV.

ZIP/POSTAL CODE

EMAIL ❏ Please check this box if you would like to receive newsletters and promotional emails from Harlequin Enterprises ULC and its affiliates. You can unsubscribe anytime.

HI/HRS-520-TY22

© 2022 HARLEQUIN ENTERPRISES ULC
™ and ® are trademarks owned by Harlequin Enterprises ULC. Printed in the U.S.A.

and dicing while tunes from her favorite playlist rose softly from her phone's speaker. She hummed along, per her usual, sampling fresh ingredients and sashaying around the little kitchen as if it was her own.

The rear deck door slid open, and she gasped. Her heart pounded and her ears rang as Nash stepped inside, phone in one hand. His gaze fell to her bare thighs, on full display beneath her favorite cotton sleep shorts, and stayed there.

She ogled his very broad, very bare chest in return. "I didn't realize you were up," she said, kicking herself for not being more aware of her surroundings. Mac Bane could have just as easily entered the kitchen, and she'd have been equally unprepared.

Nash pulled the door shut behind him and dragged his gaze to meet hers. "The phone rang, and I took the call outside so I wouldn't wake you," he explained, brows pulled low. "Did I wake you?"

"No. I was up for a while before I came out here," she said. "I didn't hear your phone."

"It was on Silent, buzzing around on my nightstand until I answered." He removed the T-shirt, which he'd hung around his neck like a towel, and fanned it out before him.

"Anything important?" she asked, returning her attention to the frittata.

"Just another round of updates." He pulled the T-shirt over his head, then slid past her in the small space to pour a cup of coffee. "It's going to be another hot one today. Still threatening to rain, but too stubborn to do it."

"Sounds like summer in Kentucky," she said. Normally, she was a dance-in-the-rain kind of girl, but suddenly she worried about how the weather would affect their visibility. Would it give Bane and his men cover? Prevent Nash and the law officers from spotting their ambush?

She removed the pan from the heat while she imagined a dozen terrible scenarios, then turned off the burner and stretched for a pair of plates. "Hungry?"

Nash's warm body grazed her back, his long arm easily passing hers as he retrieved the plates. He cradled the curve of her hip with his opposite hand, presumably to steady them. "Starving."

Fire blazed hot and fast through her veins, and a whoosh of air left her lips.

He passed her the plates with a smile.

She accepted, knowing he understood exactly what the unintentional, breathy sigh meant. He knew her too well, and she loved and hated that. "Thanks."

His eyes danced with silent delight, whether from the obvious way her body responded to his, or from the thrill it brought him as well. She couldn't be sure which was true or which she preferred as the answer.

She laughed despite herself.

They'd come to an unspoken truce over dinner, an agreement to get to know one another as they were now, without filtering their perceptions too heavily through the past. They would work together to find Bane and stay safe in the process. So all fantasies of exploring Nash's new, matured body were forbidden. She divided the frittata, plating it for them to share.

He collected forks and napkins, then accepted one plate with a playful smile. "Looks delicious."

"Thank you."

They moved to the small dinette to eat.

Nash set his phone beside his fork, screen up, so he could watch for incoming messages, as he constantly did. "It was Derek who woke me," he said. "He called to check in on you while he fed the animals. He's probably the only farmer-slash-private investigator in the state."

"You might be surprised," she said, thankful for good friends she could count on. "How'd the call go?"

"We worked through what we know about Tim and Mitchell, their friendship and immediate circle. We're trying to piece together any contacts the two might share with Bane or his known associates. We're also trying to figure out where they fit into Bane's known activities. I think you were onto something with the gambling. Cruz is reaching out to his informants today, hoping to get a bead on any new operations in the area."

Lana sipped her coffee as she listened, loading all the facts into her mind.

Nash's eyes fell shut with his first bite of breakfast. The sound that followed from his mouth was indecent.

"You like it?" she asked, smiling against the rim of her mug, indescribably pleased by his pleasure.

His lids flashed open, and he nodded slowly, taking another bite with reverence. "I forgot how good you are," he said. "This is unreal."

"It's just a frittata," she said, cheeks heating at the compliment. Cooking was something she worked hard at and was proud of. When someone noticed, it meant a lot, maybe more than it should. Coming from Nash, it was enough to make her want to combust. "Have I told you how much I appreciate the way you're including me in your investigation?" she asked, offering him a compliment in return.

His brows arched, and his expression grew serious.

She pressed on. "I realize that you could easily tell me to stay out of the way and be quiet while the professionals are at work, but you don't. You listen when I have things to say, and you fill me in on what's going on. Even when I don't completely understand what's being said, you tell me. It makes me feel less like deadweight and as if I have a measure of control in all this. It keeps me focused on a goal instead of drowning in dread, and it's probably the only reason I haven't lost my mind."

He set the fork aside and wiped a napkin over his lips. "I wish you weren't part of this. I hate that you are." His frown deepened. "I can't change that, but

I can make it manageable. I know you like staying busy, and you're smart. You know this town, and you understand people in a way I don't. Plus, you're calm under pressure and helpful. Your connection to Heidi led us to Mitchell Edwards's involvement. That connection could've taken much longer without you, and time is essential."

Her cheeks heated, and she stifled a smile.

"If you ever don't understand something," he added, "just ask. Interrupt me, and let me know. I won't mind. Everyone in my world knows what I'm saying, but it wasn't so long ago that I was scrambling to keep up. I remember not understanding. It was frustrating, and I always felt as if I was missing important pieces, running without all the facts. I haven't meant to do that to you."

Lana pursed her lips, appreciative of his patience and kindness. "Okay."

They finished their meal in companionable silence, trading furtive glances and shy smiles. Her stomach flipped and tickled with the wild butterflies of youth. The possibility that Nash sensed the same zigzagging chemistry she felt was an aphrodisiac she didn't want or need. But she enjoyed it to the fullest, anyway.

He carried their dishes to the sink when they finished.

"Do we have plans for today?" she asked, rising to join him at the counter.

He cast a cautious look over his shoulder. "Nothing definitive. Why?"

"I think we should check on Heidi," she suggested. The distressed coworker had come to mind a dozen times throughout the night and after Lana had woken. "She was pretty upset when we spoke yesterday. She thought Mitchell was at her door when we disconnected. If she's seen or spoken to him, she might know where we can find him. Or Bane."

Nash set the rinsed plates on the rack and shut off the water. "Sounds like a solid plan." He dried his hands on a dish towel as he turned to face her. "I'll let Knox know what we're getting up to and see if he or his people have questioned her yet. She's more likely to speak openly with you than the deputies either way. If she knows something that could get her friends in trouble, she'd likely hold that back from law enforcement. Maybe you can shake it loose."

Lana tipped her head. Those were her thoughts exactly. "What about you?" she asked. "Heidi doesn't know you, and she probably won't want to talk to me in front of a Marshal. Will you wait outside?"

Nash gave a dubious look. "I'm not letting you out of my sight."

She widened her eyes and lifted her palms. "Then what?"

"I won't go as a Marshal," he said, a small, conspiratorial smile on perfectly enticing lips. "I'll go as your boyfriend." He worked his brows and scooped one of her hands into his, then brought it to his chin. "If you're okay with that."

Lana made a small, unintelligible sound before snapping her mouth closed.

"Is that a *yes*?"

Lana nodded, and he brushed a gentle kiss against her knuckles.

Nash grinned. "I've always loved it when you say yes to me."

Chapter Thirteen

Nash watched Lana walk away as his phone began to buzz on the table where he'd left it. She was off to get ready for their day, and her retreat provided an incredible view. Begrudgingly, he gave up his position to answer the call. "Winchester."

"Hey," Knox returned. "I started to think you weren't going to answer. I'm not interrupting anything am I?"

Nash grinned, thinking of the easy flirtation that had developed and the way Lana had begun to let her guard down after telling him how badly he'd hurt her when he left. The confession had gutted him, but the air was beginning to clear, and that gave him hope. He still owed her a proper apology for leaving things between them the way he had when he joined the Marshals, but he had faith there would be time for that soon. As long as he didn't screw up or accidentally push her away before then. "I was just washing dishes," he told Knox, answering the nearly forgotten question. "I didn't hear the phone right away."

"Uh-huh," Knox said, sounding wholly unconvinced. "Well, if you're done doing dishes…"

"I am."

"My guys finished combing Lana's place last night," he said. "They found a few bugs."

Every muscle in Nash's body snapped to attention. "What kind of bugs?"

"Listening devices," Knox said. "We thought that might be the case yesterday but needed to get a team in there with the right equipment to perform a proper search. The devices aren't too high-tech. We're running the serial numbers to see if we can trace them back to the purchaser. My guess is that they were online purchases made via prepaid credit card, but you never know. Guys like Bane don't typically choose their lackeys based on IQ. Regardless, you should let Lana know and try to think of everything the two of you said while you were there packing her things. Chances are it was recorded."

Nash felt a bead of fury rising in him, swelling in his core and chest until he thought he'd explode. "Your team knew last night? And you're just calling now?"

A length of silence stretched over the line.

"Well, yeah," Knox said, finally. "I was trying to give you some time to sleep. You were up like forty hours straight."

Nash locked his jaw. This was the problem with working with family members. Not a single member of his team would've given two shakes how long

he was up or how tired he might be. They would've
delivered the obvious need-to-know information as
soon as they had it. But not family. Family blurred
the lines between what was acceptable on and off
the clock. They received important news, then sat
on it. So Nash could rest. He pressed angry fingers
against his temple. "Do you know how much has
transpired since Lana and I were inside her home?
How many hours? What I remember today won't be
nearly as precise or detailed as what I might've re-
membered yesterday. It's the reason we interview
witnesses at the crime scene instead of calling them
the next day," he snapped.

Knox made a huffing sound, as if he was somehow the one who was irritated.

Footfalls drew Nash's attention to the hallway,
where Lana reappeared, dark brows furrowed. "You
okay? You look like you want to hurt someone."

"Knox," he said.

"Yeah?" his cousin asked.

Lana smiled. "Carry on."

"Look," Knox said. "Just let Lana know and try
to walk back through your conversations with her.
Then let me know if either of you said anything that
could cause trouble for you now or endanger the investigation."

Nash disconnected with a grunt and quiet swear.

"Good news?" Lana asked, a teasing smile on
her lips.

He pocketed the phone and focused on Lana. Long

dark hair spilled down her back and over her shoulders. The cream-colored tank top she'd changed into looked silky. The material caressed the gentle slopes and curves of her torso, revealing teasing hints at the lace pattern in her matching bra. He let himself imagine reaching for her and pulling her against him. He could almost feel the warmth of her body and count the beats of her heart. His pulse roared at the fantasy. "Bad news," he said. "Your house was bugged. We were likely recorded while we were there, so we have to try to recall everything we said, in case any of it could become problematic for the investigation."

She leaned against the nearest wall, expression fallen and gaze fixed on the floor. "At least no one else is dead," she said, then frowned. "Wow. The bar for what's acceptable has really lowered."

He smiled. "Let's get out of here. We can talk in the car."

Lana lifted her eyes and chin. "Still playing the role of my boyfriend?"

"If that's still all right," he said.

She offered him her hand.

The drive to Heidi's home was tense for new reasons, as their hands lay joined on the seat between them. Nash checked the rearview mirror for signs of a tail and kept watch over the other cars moving along in traffic. He squeezed Lana's fingers every few minutes to be sure he wasn't imagining their physical connection.

He'd sent a text on their way out the door, letting Knox know where they were headed and why. Once Lana took a crack at playing the friend card to get Heidi to open up, Knox could take his turn with the deputy card. Trusted friends could loosen lips, but so could a properly applied badge where amateurs were concerned, and from what Lana had said, Heidi seemed to be unsuspecting and innocent.

Lana's phone rang, and she released his hand in favor of lifting the device to her ear. "Hi, Mama," she said, smiling cautiously.

Nash tried not to listen too carefully as Lana gave her mom a loose rundown of the situation. She purposefully skipped the parts where she was involved in anything dangerous and stuck to the fact Nash was in town chasing a fugitive, who'd since killed her boss. Several minutes passed before Lana convinced her mom she was safe and happy and that she'd call again as soon as she could.

"That went well," Nash said, sliding his eyes in her direction.

"I didn't want to worry her," Lana said, "but I don't think I reached that goal. She's probably buying two plane tickets to Kentucky as we speak."

Nash grinned.

Lana leaned forward, straining against her seat belt as Heidi's street drew near. "This is it," she said. "The sign's barely visible in front of that tree. Right after this gray house and the red hatchback."

"Got it." He slowed to take the turn as instructed.

The neighborhood was newer, with small homes and big yards. The kind of place where residents raised families, small livestock and large dogs. Uncut fields of grass and wildflowers stretched between properties. Outbuildings and swing sets peppered the landscape.

"Heidi saved forever to buy a home here," Lana said. "She has these lawn chickens named after old country-music stars and takes pictures of them as if they're her kids."

Nash smiled at the idea and Lana's dry tone. "You don't like yard chickens?"

"Of course I do," she said, returning his smile. "I don't have a yard for them yet, but I will."

It was true. Her town house was bookended by identical structures. The front and backyards were minuscule and overtaken by small porches and patios.

"I still live in an apartment," he said. "Small and efficient." To accommodate his harried work schedule and cheap enough to pay extra rent in advance when he and his team were out of town for long stretches.

"A bachelor pad," she said. "That sounds about right. Tell me you don't drink from plastic party cups and eat leftover pizza more than once a week."

He frowned, and she laughed.

He really did need to get a bigger place. Maybe a home with a lawn to mow. Maybe a family to fill it with joy and laughter. The idea stunned him silent.

"You okay?" Lana asked. "You look pale."

He'd always wanted a family, but he was never ready for the time and effort that kind of responsibility would take. His job had to come first while he established himself with the Marshals. He'd done that, but hadn't given a family much thought in years. Why was he thinking about it now? Was he ready now? He'd assumed that something would click or change internally one day, and he'd just...know. Was that what this meant? Was he ready for a family? Now?

A deputy's cruiser came into view at the end of the block, yanking him away from the strange thought.

Next, he noticed the ambulance.

"Oh, no," Lana whispered, turning her attention to the emergency vehicles as well.

The scene they were rolling up on wasn't a good one, and it seemed to be taking place outside their intended destination.

"That's Heidi's house," Lana whispered.

A woman stood on the sidewalk with a uniformed deputy. Tears and mascara streamed over her cheeks.

"Tell me that's Heidi," Nash said, slowing to a stop in the middle of the road.

"It's not Heidi," she said.

He released a slow breath, unsure parking outside a crime scene was a great idea. If anyone on Bane's team was watching, they'd recognize Lana and make note of the truck. That would be bad news for them later.

Knox appeared on the home's porch, then jogged down the sidewalk, past the crying woman and other deputy. He scowled and swung his arm in a large circle, demanding Nash move on.

Nash powered the window down and lifted his chin.

His cousin's expression darkened to a heated scowl. "Get moving," he called, pointing them furiously away. "There's nothing to see here."

Lana leaned across the bench seat in Nash's direction, chewing her bottom lip and tracking Knox with her eyes. "Is Heidi okay?" she called, the moment he was close enough to hear.

Knox gave a small shake of his head, then finished the walk to Nash's window. "The neighbor came over because Heidi's dog had been barking," he said, voice low and gaze drifting over the larger scene. "The door was ajar when she got here, so she called Dispatch. Emergency Services probably took the call around the same time I was on the line with you," he told Nash. "I came over the minute I got word."

The grim set of his features told Nash the rest of the story.

"But she's not hurt?" Lana said, apparently mistaking the intention of Knox's earlier headshake.

His expression turned deeply remorseful. "I'm sorry, Lana," he told her. "Heidi was in bad shape when first responders arrived." He looked over his shoulder as the home's door opened behind him.

"There wasn't much they could do. Now, you guys need to go before you're identified."

Knox stepped back and swung his arm again. "Keep moving!"

Nash released the brake pedal as paramedics piloted a gurney to the ambulance, a sealed body bag on top.

Chapter Fourteen

Lana watched in horror as EMTs loaded the gurney into the ambulance. She craned her neck and twisted in her seat as the crime scene behind them became a smudge of blue and red light in the distance and the ambulance trundled silently away, having no reason to scream or hurry.

She righted herself with a shuddered breath and adjusted her seat belt. Her skin tingled, and her breaths were strained. The horror of seeing the body bag, and knowing Heidi was inside, was too much. Too shocking. Too incomprehensibly awful. And Lana was going numb.

Nash drove around the block, then down an alley and back up, seeming to go nowhere.

For a moment, she wondered if he'd been shocked temporarily senseless too.

He parked behind a church and set his phone on the dashboard, then tapped the screen.

Lana waited, unsure her voice would be there if she called upon it. Her breaths were too shallow and uneven. Her racing heart thudded in her ears. The numbness had spread into a strange, out-of-body sensation.

Knox's face appeared on Nash's phone screen. He strode through Heidi's home and onto the porch. Emergency responders crisscrossed the scene behind him, moving in and out of the open front door.

Lana's stomach pitted, and her head lightened.

"Hey," Nash said, adjusting the phone's camera angle. "We're at the church about three blocks away. I wanted to get the rundown. Some cop rushed me off at the scene."

Knox gave a bland expression. "You know whoever did this is watching from somewhere, right?"

"Probably," Nash admitted. "You were smart to run me off. I wasn't complaining."

"For the record, I'm a deputy sheriff, not a cop, but I suppose Marshals don't have time to worry about the differences," Knox said.

Nash smiled. "Tell me what you know, Deputy."

Lana listened to the garbled conversation, attempting to anchor herself to the familiar voices and push through the shock. *The Winchesters are accustomed to death and trauma*, she reminded herself. *They hadn't known Heidi or Tim.* The Winchesters were fine. Lana was not.

She powered her window down to get more air.

"The victim was shot in the back," Knox said. "Sometime late yesterday afternoon."

Lana's stomach lurched, and she locked her teeth together.

"Blood spatter suggests she was running when it happened."

Lana turned to face the phone, a single word stuck in her mind. "Running?"

Nash adjusted the phone to put Lana's image on-screen for his cousin.

Knox nodded. "I'm sorry for your loss."

She took a small breath and tested her voice once more. "Was she running away from the front door?"

"It appears that way." Knox frowned. "How did you know?"

Lana set a trembling hand over her lips as Heidi's voice returned to her.

"There's someone at my door. I'm going to have to go. It's probably Mickey. He'll want to talk, and I could use the company."

Nash leaned in her direction, bringing himself into the frame. "Lana was on the phone with Heidi yesterday, around your estimated time of death. She ended the call to answer the door. She thought it was Mitchell Edwards."

"It might've been," Knox said. "No one knows where he is or what he's up to. Maybe he was covering his own tracks or tying up loose ends. Maybe Heidi was one of them."

Lana dropped her hands into her lap, aghast. "Why would someone do this to her?"

Nash offered her a solemn look. "She told you

Tim had been spending a lot of time on the boat with Mitchell lately. Maybe that knowledge was enough. If one was guilty, I'm betting the other was tied to the crime somehow, whatever it is. Knox is right. Mitchell could've been making sure there wasn't anyone to testify against him when it all came out."

"Lana," Knox said, "how close were Heidi and Tim?"

She scanned a thousand fuzzy memories in search of the most accurate answer. "They've been off and on for a while, but they're close. And she told me he'd recently asked her to run away with him."

Knox nodded. "Was she close to Mitchell too?"

Lana frowned. "As friends?"

"You tell me," he said. "I'm just trying to get an idea of how much these men might've told her."

"I don't know," Lana admitted. "She didn't talk to me about her personal life." And given how much she hadn't known about Tim and Mitchell, she was beginning to wonder if she really knew anyone.

Nash reached for her hand, pulling it onto the bench between them, outside the camera's view. "He's running the probability of various scenarios," Nash said. "It helps form a narrative and gives investigators a place to begin. If Heidi and Mitchell were close, romantically or otherwise, Bane and his men would know. And if Mitchell took off before Bane reached him, they might've gone to Heidi to demand his location."

"Or," Knox said, "they might've wanted to use

Heidi as leverage to bring Mitchell back from wherever he went."

Lana turned her palm beneath Nash's, spreading her fingers and urging his between. When he folded his hand over hers once more, she found renewed strength in the touch. "You said she ran after answering the door, and she was shot in the back?"

"We believe so," Knox agreed. "But there aren't any signs of forced entry or indication regarding the amount of time that transpired between her answering the door and being attacked. She could've invited her killer in or been tricked into opening up. There's a lot we can't know."

Nash gave Lana's fingers a reassuring squeeze. "Any signs of a struggle inside?"

Knox's brows rose, and he began to nod. "Significant evidence suggests the victim knew she was in trouble before she ran. There were a number of defensive wounds on her person as well as a destroyed foyer, in an otherwise-organized home." He spoke more quietly to another deputy before returning his attention to the camera. "A second source of blood suggests she got in a few good hits before attempting to make her escape. The lab will run the blood sample with tissue found under her nails and any hairs or fibers on her clothes and skin. They'll do their best to put a name with whoever did this. Ballistics is working with the casings found on scene. They'll try to match them to the gun used in the attack. If the gun has been used in another crime, we

can connect the cases, victims and suspects, then
go from there."

Someone called Knox's name in the background,
and he turned in response. "On my way," he answered, before looking back at the screen. "We've
got things covered here. I highly recommend you
guys go to the safe house and lie low."

Lana released a ragged breath, hating that Heidi
had died alone, afraid and under attack. But strangely
thankful she'd fought back. The DNA found on her
could be the thing that put her killer behind bars.

"Anything else before we go?" Nash asked.

"That's all we know so far," Knox said. "Except
we haven't been able to locate a cell phone or laptop." His gaze shifted to Lana. "Any idea where she
might've kept those? We've checked her house and
car. Did she have a locker at work or a gym she fre-
quented?"

Lana chewed her lip, easily recalling the bedaz-
zled case on Heidi's phone and the smattering of local
band stickers on her computer. "I've seen her with
both," she said. "But I don't know where they'd be."

"Killer probably took them," Nash said.

Knox nodded. "I'm hoping they're just somewhere
safe for now. Meanwhile, we're setting up to sweep
for listening devices. We'll keep you posted."

"Thanks," Nash said. "We'll do the same."

Lana tugged his hand as something new came to
mind. "There was a laptop on the desk in the living
room at Mitchell's place."

Nash's eyes flashed with interest. "We'll pick that up while you finish there, then touch base afterward."

Knox pursed his lips. His gaze shifted from Nash to Lana and back. "Maybe you should just head back to the safe house. I can have Dispatch send a unit to Edwards's place."

Lana bristled, overwhelmed by the need to take action the way Heidi had. "We can do this," she said. "I know right where it is. I can be in and out before anyone else has a chance to show up and take it." Assuming no one had already broken in and done that.

An unexpected smile curved one side of Nash's mouth. "I'll give you a call when we have the device," he told Knox. "Let tech services know we'll be bringing the laptop to the sheriff's department."

Knox stared through the screen, pointedly displeased.

"I've got this," Nash assured him, clearly not asking for his cousin's permission or blessing. "Tell tech we'll be there soon."

"Yeah," Knox said, running a hand through messy hair. "Be careful, and stay in touch. If I don't hear back from you in thirty minutes, I'm going to assume something bad is going on and send the entire department in your direction."

"Appreciated," Nash said.

Lana forced a tight smile. "Thank you."

Knox groaned. "For the record, I don't like this. But if you happen to run into Mitchell Edwards, don't let him leave."

"Not my first rodeo," Nash said, tapping the screen to disconnect the call. He tossed the phone into the cup holder. "Let's go."

Lana folded her hands on her lap, nerves jangled, but hope rising. "Do you think Mitchell will be there this time?"

"I doubt it," Nash said. "He left in a hurry. I don't see him coming back anytime soon. Though I have a feeling he could cut my time chasing Bane in half if he was around to question."

All the more reason to stay hidden, Lana thought. Everyone who knew anything about Bane was fast turning up dead.

NASH POINTED THE truck in the direction of Mitchell Edwards's home and pressed the accelerator. He hoped, for Mitchell's sake, that he was a good hider, because it seemed as if the circle of friends he'd known and trusted was slowly being erased.

The drive was short and uneventful, no signs of a tail and very little traffic. Nash counted it all as good fortune and hoped the pattern would continue. He parked the truck on the curb across the street from Mitchell's home and gave the scene a careful examination before climbing out. He met Lana at the front bumper, one hand extended.

She set her palm on his, and he pulled her close to his side.

"Let's be quick," he said, breaking into a jog.

Lana had no trouble keeping up as they crossed

the street, then ran alongside the home to the back of the house.

"Where are we going?" she asked.

Nash lifted the doormat on Mitchell's back porch in answer. He turned it upside down, and a key spilled out. "I put this aside in case we needed it again."

"You stole his key?"

"No," he said. "I moved it from the rack inside to this mat in case we needed to get back in here. And we do, so yay."

Lana rolled her eyes, and Nash slipped the relocated key into the door lock.

He felt the tumbler turn and breathed easier. This was officially a good-luck streak.

Lana stepped inside ahead of him, then waited in the kitchen, while he pulled the door shut.

Nash took the lead through the house, listening for signs they weren't alone.

His gaze fell on the living-room desk as they entered the room. The laptop was exactly where they'd left it. "Grab his phone if you see it."

Lana moved to collect the device, while Nash made his rounds, checking for forced entry or intruders. "I've got the computer," she said, unplugging the device from the wall and gathering the cord. "No phone."

"All right." Nash returned to her quickly. He hadn't seen a cell phone either, but he was thankful for what they had. "I'll let Knox know." He tapped the message into his phone, as he followed her onto the back porch.

She locked up and returned the key to under the doormat. "Ready."

They made the return trip along the side of the house at a much slower pace, while Nash fielded messages from his team and the local deputies. The contents of the laptop were sure to provide a clue about Bane's presence in Great Falls, and Mitchell's connection to it. Even when people thought they'd deleted condemning materials online or tossed documents in the digital trash, nothing like that was ever really gone. Not when your tech team was good enough.

Given the excellent string of luck Nash was having, he had no doubt the cyber specialists in town would be top-tier.

"Nash," Lana said, tugging a handful of his shirt as they reached the front lawn.

He pulled his eyes from the phone to her ghost-white expression, and fear raced like ice through his veins. "What's wrong?" He followed her wide-eyed gaze to a navy-blue sedan moving down the street in their direction, Pennsylvania license plates visible on the front.

"That's the car from outside the restaurant," she whispered. "It's Bane's car."

Her words were nearly drowned out by the fierce squealing of tires on asphalt as the car barreled suddenly forward. A gun appeared through the open driver's-side window as the car passed before them. And a spray of gunfire ensued.

"Get down!" Nash ordered, already too late. He threw himself over Lana, knocking her to the ground in a heap of grunts and tangle of limbs.

They collided with the rain-starved earth in a bone-jarring thud, before skidding to a painful stop against the home's brick base.

The car's tires squealed again, and Nash leaped to his feet.

He freed his gun and took aim at shrinking taillights while the sedan raced away, carrying the gunman with it.

Lana remained motionless at his feet, a trail of blood stretching across her cheek.

Chapter Fifteen

Sirens wailed in the distance as Nash examined Lana's limp form and lax face.

His heart hammered and his lungs ached with every new and labored breath, while Lana's chest rose and fell in brief, barely visible motions. She was hurt, and it was his fault. He'd dived at her, knocking her across the lawn several feet before they'd collided with the ground, then with the house. He'd done his best to take the brunt of the impact for them both, but he'd been hasty and had acted on instinct, sparing no time for forethought.

Lana's limbs twitched, and her nose wrinkled.

He sighed in relief, thankful beyond measure for her reanimation. She'd only been unconscious for a minute, but he'd imagined a thousand terrible outcomes in that time.

"Lana," he whispered. "You're okay. I'm here." He pushed dark, tangled hair away from her forehead and cheeks, careful not to move her head or neck. The blood seemed to be coming from a cut above her eyebrow.

Her eyelids fluttered open, and she reached for him. "Nash."

"Hey," he said, blissful and dizzy from the sound of his name on her tongue. "I've got you."

Lana slid her fingers around his biceps and urged him closer. "Are you okay?" she asked.

"I'm fine," he reassured her, setting his forehead briefly against hers. "You need to be still until the ambulance arrives. I called Dispatch, and help is on the way."

"I'm okay," she repeated, squirming as if she might get up.

He hovered over her, one arm on each side of her chest, locking her in place. "Not a chance. You could have a concussion or internal bleeding. Stay here with me a few more minutes."

Sirens drew closer, and he breathed a little easier still. "Hear that? Help is almost here."

Lana set a palm against his stubbled cheek. "You saved my life."

"I knocked you down. You lost consciousness," he said, pulling back to frown. "You're bleeding because of me."

Lana tented her brows and smiled. "I'm alive because of you." She slid her hands over his shoulders, to the back of his neck and tugged him closer. "You threw yourself in front of bullets for me."

Nash stiffened. He had done that, but it wasn't

even a choice. He would always protect her, from anything or anyone. Whatever the cost.

"I've missed you," she whispered, dark, sexy eyes searching his.

He blinked, thoroughly rattled by the unexpected confession, and wondering if, perhaps, he was the one with a head injury.

She missed him?

She should hate him. He'd chosen a job over her, or at least that had been her perception of the decision. And he hadn't stuck around to set her straight.

Around them, a crowd of Mitchell's neighbors began to form. Their hurried voices united in a chorus of buzzing sound. Some called out the street name, as if trying to triangulate help. Others raised their phones in Nash and Lana's direction, taking video or snapping photos.

Nash turned his back to them, raising his badge in one hand overhead.

A moment later, the screaming sirens arrived. Ambulances, cruisers and a fire truck.

News trucks wouldn't be far behind.

Nash's cousin, Isaac, was the first EMT to reach them. He set his medical kit in the grass and looked from Nash to Lana. "You were shot at."

"I know," she said, a croak of emotion in her tone.

He pinned Nash with an accusatory stare. "She was shot at."

"I'm aware," Nash said. "I think she hit her head when she fell."

Lana raised a palm to her hair. "Here."

Isaac went to work, and Nash peeled himself away, cradling his bruised abs in one arm.

The laptop they'd come for, and he'd temporarily forgotten in the chaos, lay in the grass several yards away, propelled from Lana's hands in the fall. The lid was slightly askew.

He stretched onto his feet and went to retrieve the device, hoping more than ever that the Great Falls Sheriff's Department had a really good tech team.

He returned with the laptop and sat beside Lana with a soft hiss.

"Ribs hurt?" Isaac guessed, eyeballing the arm across Nash's middle. "I hear you took another blow to that general area not long ago. You want me to take a look when I finish here?"

"I'm fine," Nash said. "It's nice to see you again, man." He stretched his arms out, fist curled, to air-bump his younger cousin's gloved hand.

Isaac smiled. "Wish we could meet up under better conditions. What's that about?" He flashed a pen into Lana's eyes, then worked his gloved hands over her head and through her hair.

"It's the Winchester way," Nash said, laughing gently, then wincing at the pain.

Isaac rolled his eyes. "Someone needs to plan a reunion like normal families. We could eat barbecue and play lawn games instead of always chasing bad guys and patching up the good ones."

"Good luck with that," Lana said. "None of you guys would come."

Isaac grinned. "You're probably right. Any tenderness here?" he asked, probing the cut above her brow.

"Ow," she said.

"I'm going to clean and bandage it. Any nausea? Blurry vision?"

Lana shook her head. "None."

"Additional pains?"

"Yeah," she said flatly. "Everywhere."

Nash grimaced, and Isaac gave him a pointed stare.

"Well, a giant fell on you," Isaac said. "I suppose that's to be expected." He finished applying the bandage, then stood and offered Lana his hand. "On your feet. Let's see how you do."

Isaac looked to Nash once more. "What were the two of you doing here, anyway?"

Nash rose to join them. "We were retrieving this laptop."

But they should've gone back to the safe house like Knox suggested.

As if on cue, Knox's cruiser tore into position beside the ambulance. He jumped out and dashed across the lawn to Lana. "What the heck!" he yelled, directing the venom at Nash, then swinging his eyes to Isaac. "Is she okay?"

Lana offered an unenthusiastic wave. "We got the laptop."

Knox scowled. "You were shot at."

Nash handed the computer to his cousin, ignoring the statement.

Knox swore. The lid was too beat-up from the fall to fully close. Tufts of mud and grass clung to the hinges and keyboard. "Are you kidding me? I knew you should've gone back to the safe house. I should've insisted. Instead, you were both nearly killed, and the laptop is probably ruined."

Lana's expression went hard, then sour. "If we hadn't come here when we did, you wouldn't have that laptop at all," she said, sounding more like herself than she had since the fall. "Bane was probably on his way here to break in and take it, along with who knows what else."

"He shot at you," Knox said, getting equally riled. "You shouldn't be part of this investigation. You're a witness under federal protection. You're supposed to be out of sight and safe. In the safe house."

Lana chewed her lip, the bluster knocked out of her. "Would it really matter where we were?" she asked, her tone defeated. "He found me here. How long will it be before he finds me there too?"

Nash moved to her side. Gone was the dreamy expression she'd worn only moments before, while looking into his eyes, and present was the terror of someone whose life was in immediate and constant danger.

He hated himself for not being better at his job.

Knox raised a hand in surrender. "I'm sorry this happened," he said. "I'm glad you're okay."

Her eyes filled with unshed tears. "Thank you."

Isaac hung his stethoscope around his neck and grinned. "Her heart's racing and her pulse is understandably high, but she doesn't appear to have any substantive injuries. I anticipate some bruising and tenderness, but nothing an over-the-counter painkiller and ice won't help."

"See?" Lana said. "I'm fine. And I'm ready to get out of here."

Nash set a palm against her back and traced small circles with his thumb. His gaze fell to the battered laptop in Knox's grip, and something of interest came to mind. "You were talking to us from Heidi's home when we decided to come here," he said. "I think it's safe to say there are bugs at her place too."

Knox nodded. "I thought the same thing when I heard Dispatch announce shots were fired at this address."

"Can we be sure the safe house hasn't been compromised?" Nash asked. And if not, where would they go?

Knox tapped his phone screen. "Let's touch base with Cruz and Derek on that. Have you had a chance to think about what the two of you said while you were at Lana's place? Did you give any indication about the location where you're staying?"

Nash's gaze drifted to Lana, who stared up at him

with wide, uncertain eyes. "I don't know," he admitted. "We still need to go over that."

"Make it a priority," Knox said. His phone buzzed, and he looked at the screen. "Meanwhile, Cruz is on his way to the house to scan for bugs. He says they can relocate you, if needed. Auntie Rosa and Uncle Hank will help."

Isaac nodded. "They're excellent at this kind of thing."

Lana fixed Isaac with a curious stare. "Do they have a lot of opportunities to get involved?"

He gave a humorless laugh. "More than you'd think."

Nash shook hands with each of his cousins. "We'll wait for word from Derek before we head back," he said. "Meanwhile, I want to get Lana out of here."

She leaned against his side as they moved away from the scene, and his long-tightened heart unfurled.

Lana had said she'd missed him.

Chapter Sixteen

Lana rubbed her neck, which had started to ache, while Nash drove aimlessly along the outskirts of Great Falls and into neighboring towns, wasting time until Cruz had a chance to check the safe house for bugs or signs of unwanted visitors. "Can we pull over somewhere?" she asked, a little nauseous from the dying rush of adrenaline. "I think I need some fresh air and maybe a walk to stretch."

Her tangled thoughts and racing heart made it hard to find equilibrium. The shooting outside Mitchell's house had complicated her already-miserable day. Heidi was gone. Killed while she'd run for her life. Bane had pulled a gun on Lana and Nash in broad daylight. Someone had shot Nash's SUV the day before, also in the middle of the day, and Bane had pushed Tim off a roof. The safe, small town she loved was filling with criminals, gunfire and murder. Lana wasn't sure her heart could take whatever came next.

Nash hit his turn signal and slowed.

An ice-cream stand appeared in the distance, partially wrapped in a U-shaped parking lot and situated across the road from a small riverfront park.

A massive sign, shaped like a twist cone and outlined in neon lights, topped the building. A queue of customers placed orders at a sliding glass window, then carried their treats to a smattering of tables with umbrellas, to their cars or across the street to the park.

"What do you think?" Nash asked.

Lana smiled. "I think I'm glad I didn't ask you to stop a few minutes ago when I saw a gas station advertising rotisserie hot dogs."

Nash laughed. "Let's get milkshakes and fries, then walk over there to eat." He pointed to the paved walkway lined in leafy trees beside the water. Wooden and wrought iron benches nestled in shady places every few dozen yards.

"That sounds perfect."

Nash parked in the lot, then turned to her with a serious stare.

"This wasn't your fault," she said, climbing out before he could argue.

Lana ordered a bottle of water, unsure her churning stomach could handle anything more substantial. Nash ordered a milkshake and a basket of fries as promised.

When their orders were filled, they crossed the street to the park.

Lana chose a bench in the shade of an ancient oak tree, and Nash took a seat at her side. Slowly, her pulse began to settle, and peace filtered over her as she enjoyed each cool sip from her bottle.

Nash stretched his long legs out before him and hooked one elbow over the bench's back support. His squinted eyes stared out across the water.

She thought of the way he'd thrown himself in front of her, protecting her from gunfire, and the way he'd worried for her while they'd waited for the EMTs. "I wanted to kiss you," she said, without any real intention. The thought entered her head only a moment before the words were on her tongue. Her cheeks heated, but she squared her shoulders and owned the confession.

It wasn't the sort of thing she'd normally say, even if it was true. But her time felt short, and the need to be truthful, both to Nash and to herself, seemed infinitely more important than anything else.

In that moment, on Mitchell's lawn, she'd been certain Nash had wanted to kiss her too.

His chewing slowed, and he swallowed before turning to face her. But he didn't speak.

"Did you want to kiss me?" she asked.

His soulful blue eyes roamed her face, and she wished she could read the emotion she saw there.

"I did," he said softly.

Lana released a short puff of air. Relief mixed with awe. And maybe a little hope. "Why?" she asked.

"What do you mean?" He set his fries and shake aside. "Why did I want to kiss you?"

She nodded. "Was it because you wanted to calm

me down? Because I was freaking out? Was it the adrenaline rush? A result of the heightened emotions?"

Nash frowned. "I'm so sorry. It was terrible timing, and I realize it probably seemed as if I was going to take advantage of a bad situation. You just caught me off guard, saying you missed me." He cringed. "I owe you an apology."

Lana turned away. Nash was sorry. He was a nice man who didn't really want to kiss her and regretted having thought about it. She stifled a deep internal groan.

"I could've lost you," he whispered.

Her gaze flickered back to him. "You left me eight years ago," she said. "I'm not angry anymore. I'm just saying I haven't been yours to lose in a long time." The words sounded cold to her ears, and the familiar sting of building tears pricked her eyes.

His expression darkened, and his jaw clenched. "I was young, prideful and stupid. You deserved better."

"I deserved an explanation," she said. "I deserved closure. I spent months wondering what I could've done differently. Not understanding how I was happy and you were ready to catch the next bus out of town."

Nash pulled his head back, as if he'd been slapped. "I checked in on you through my cousins. They assured me you were happy. You were building a life and a career, managing just fine, probably better with me gone."

"Because I told them to say it," she said. "I didn't

want you to think I was here, floundering, piecing
my heart back together while you moved on."

Nash rubbed a heavy hand over his mouth. He
took his time before speaking. An infuriating habit
she always appreciated once the wait was over. Nash
Winchester always considered his words, and he
never said anything he didn't mean. It was a trait
shared by very few people. Herself included. How
many times lately had she told him she was fine?
It hadn't been true once. "I planned to propose the
night I told you I got the job with the Marshals," he
said.

Lana's mouth opened, and she had to force it shut.

"We'd been fighting more often that summer because I was being secretive and shutting you down
when you asked about it. I think you thought I was
cheating, but I was interviewing in Louisville, and I
didn't want you to know unless I got the job. I'd told
you on the night we met that being a Marshal was
my goal, and I didn't want you to know if I failed. I
wanted you to be proud of me." He swallowed, and
his Adam's apple bobbed.

Lana exhaled, long and slow. She had wondered
if he was cheating. He'd been distant and squirrelly,
not like the man who'd stolen her heart. But she'd
also watched him become more restless and detached
for nearly a year at that point, and she'd wondered
if he was okay. He'd only pushed her further away
when she'd asked.

"I'd missed fighting for something. Serving my

country and making a difference. I needed to be a Marshal like I needed air. But I was young and high-strung and far less mature than you were, even though I was four years older, and when my good news turned into an argument, I lashed out for absolutely no reason. I expected you to read my mind and understand all the things I hadn't said. Like how being a Marshal was going to give me the purpose I'd lacked for so long and make me feel like I was someone who could set goals and reach them."

Lana's heart pounded, and her skin began to feel too tight. Memories of their last days together, coupled with his explanation, made her hackles rise. She had been proud of him. He'd served his country, honored his family and loved her. He was pursuing his dreams by interviewing with the Marshals. What part of that did he think wasn't worthy of her pride? Her frown deepened, and words bottlenecked in her throat.

He'd planned to marry her, but instead he'd broken her heart.

Nash's phone rang, and he freed it from his pocket. "It's the marina office," he said. "I guess they got my business card." He stood to take the call, putting intentional distance between himself and Lana for the first time since his return to her life.

She chugged the remainder of her water, trying not to imagine what the last eight years would've been for her if Nash had proposed instead of storming off. They would've had a home together and built a life. They might even have babies by now.

Or, she thought dryly, they might've been divorced, because he clearly hadn't been ready for any of that.

For the first time in all those years, she saw the Nash who'd walked away from her in a much dimmer light. She'd seen his heart and known his potential, but he'd hidden the insecure and imperfect parts of himself. And she'd deserved a man who bared everything to her and trusted her to accept it. Ugly parts and all.

Nash tucked the phone into his pocket and headed back to the bench. "Sorry about that. The office manager at the marina says Mitchell Edwards took *Sandy* out yesterday afternoon, but he hasn't seen him or the boat since. He's going to keep watch and notify the sheriff's department if either show up." Nash collected his shake and the nearly empty basket of fries, then tossed them in the nearest receptacle.

Lana rose to meet him in the grass. "Do we have time to walk before we go?"

He offered her his hand, expression warm, but vulnerable. "Sure."

She slid her fingers over his. "I wish you would've told me you were miserable back then," she said, heart breaking a little with the words.

Nash glanced down at her. "I knew you'd think you were the cause, or that there was something you could do to fix me. The truth was, I'd been restless a long time, and I didn't feel settled again until I became a Marshal. Protecting and serving is in my blood. It feels good and right. Waiting tables, working in offices—none of that felt right. And no matter how much I loved you, you weren't going to fill that void for me. If I'd been half the man you deserved, I'd have told you that, and we'd have made a plan to figure it out together. Instead, I announced I got the job and was moving, then asked you to come along, and I managed to be hurt when you didn't think that was a supreme and fantastic offer."

She smiled. "I get it, you know. If I couldn't cook, I'd feel the same. For the record, you should only apologize for wanting to kiss me today if you were truly just planning to take advantage of my vulnerable state," she said.

Nash made a soft, snorting sound, as they fell into a meandering pace along the waterfront.

"I know that wasn't your intent," she said, "because you'd never take advantage of anyone or anything. So we're good. Unless you think I should apologize for wanting to kiss you."

Nash stopped walking and released her hand. "Were you planning to take advantage of me?"

She laughed. "No."

"Never be sorry for wanting to kiss me," he said.

The small waver in his voice melted her heart.

"I like kissing you," she whispered. "It's been a long time, but I remember."

Nash's eyes narrowed, and his phone rang. She pressed her lips together and smiled.

He glanced, begrudgingly, at the screen. "That's my team."

She waited while Nash relayed the morning's events to whoever was on the other end of the line. He told them about the safe house's possible breach and the potential relocation. When he finished, he put the phone away and reached for her.

"Let's head back into town and see if Cruz or Derek have any new information," he said. "My team will be here in a few hours, and they need to know where they're headed."

Lana walked back across the street to Nash's truck, immeasurably thankful his team was on the way. More officials on the case would likely mean catching Bane sooner. And she needed her life out of danger ASAP. Because as soon as she knew it was safe to distract him, Lana was going to kiss Nash Winchester like she meant it and hope he meant it too.

NASH PARKED OUTSIDE his cousins' PI office with renewed hope. His team was finally on their way, which meant more protection for Lana. And she'd wanted to kiss him today. Maybe his luck was getting back on track.

"Ready?" he asked.

"Yep," she answered, already reaching for her door handle.

He met her on the sidewalk, pride swelling as she took his hand.

Derek opened the office door as they approached, then stood back to let them pass. His gaze dropped immediately to their joined hands, and his eyes narrowed.

Nash gave a small shake of his head in warning.

Derek shook his head in return.

"Well, look at the two of you," Cruz announced, slapping his palms together. "Seems like you finally made up."

Lana's cheeks turned pink, and Nash squeezed her hand in silent reassurance.

Cruz's smile grew. "I'm right. Right?" he asked. "Is it a secret? Because holding hands in public is a dead giveaway."

"Shut up, dork," Lana said.

Derek barked out a laugh, and Nash let the moment of levity rise.

They followed Cruz to his desk and sat in the chairs across from him.

Nash set his left ankle on his right knee and did his best to look more confident than he felt. "Did one of you have the chance to check out the safe house?"

"Yeah," Cruz said. "I just got back and was relaying the details to Derek when we saw you pull up."

Lana's eyes widened. "And?"

"All clear," he said. "No bugs, no signs of forced entry or lookie-loos. I think the place is safe for now. We'll leave it up to you if you want to move."

Nash shifted forward on his seat, resting his elbows on his thighs and steepling his fingers. "My team's on the way," he said. "They'll be in town soon. I'll let them know we might be moving to a new location, but we'll meet at the safe house for now."

Derek moved to the business side of the second desk and gripped the wireless mouse. He gave the device a few clicks, then looked to his partner. "Old Smokey?"

Cruz swiped a baseball from the inside of his overturned ball cap and tossed it into the air. "That could work." He caught the ball and threw it again. "I'd add a lookout."

"I can make that happen," Derek said. "The family cabin isn't too far away."

Lana wrinkled her nose. "Hold on. What's Old Smokey?"

Cruz grinned. "An historic but updated log cabin at the top of Great Mountain. We bought the property at a steal, but the first time Derek made a fire without checking the flue we had some heavy smoke damage. The associated repair costs made up for the initial savings."

Derek made a face. "You always have to tell that story."

"Yes, I do." Cruz tossed the ball again, clearly proud of himself.

Nash wasn't sold on a historic cabin. "How many beds?" If his team stayed with them, that meant four grown men, and one witness sharing a space.

"Six," Cruz said. "Three bedrooms. Two cots in each."

"Wi-Fi and cell reception are spotty," Derek added. "It's better at the family cabin, but that can be traced to us. This can't. The two are only a mile or so apart as the crow flies. You could travel between the two in a pinch."

Nash gripped the back of his neck where tension had gathered once more. His mind easily inserted *in case of attack* where Derek had said *in a pinch*.

Derek opened a desk drawer and retrieved a key from a box with a half dozen similar items. "If you need it, it's yours," he said, passing the key into Nash's hand. "I'll post up on the main road nearby and keep watch on passing vehicles. I'll let you know if anything seems off. Just let me know before you head out, if that's what you decide to do."

Nash pocketed the key. "Thanks. We'll be in touch."

Now it was time to meet the team.

Chapter Seventeen

Lana paced the floor of the small white safe house, anxious to meet the members of Nash's team. These were the people he spent his time with now. These were the men who knew him best, and she hoped, nonsensically, that they would like her.

She poured a glass of water and peeked through the front curtain for the dozenth time, certain she'd heard the sound of tires on gravel. But like every other time, she was wrong.

"They made it," Nash said, returning from his bedroom, where he'd gone to change his grass-stained clothes, following the tumble on Mitchell's lawn. "They're getting gas now and will be here in a minute."

"Good," she said, drinking him in and appreciating their final moments alone.

She'd swapped her previous outfit for yoga pants and a tank top, choosing comfort over fashion. Her body was too sore to deal with buttons or zippers.

"You look nervous," he said, joining her at the

window. "Don't be. I trust Cruz and Derek. If they say it's safe here, I believe them."

Lana rolled her eyes up to meet his gaze, enjoying the way his broad frame loomed over hers. "Do you think your team will like me?" she asked. "I don't know how long we'll all have to live together, and I'm wondering what happens if they think I'm the worst."

Nash chuckled. "No one would think you're the worst. You're great." He cradled the back of her head in one large hand and pulled her against his chest.

Her arms wrapped around him on instinct, and she melted into the embrace.

The sound of an approaching vehicle drew her eyes to the driveway once more. A dark SUV, like the one Nash had arrived in, crawled slowly in their direction.

"Speak of the devils," Nash said, pulling back to reveal a broad smile. He opened the front door, as three men exited the vehicle.

The foursome traded handshakes and awkward one-arm hugs.

She watched from the open doorway, not wanting to rush out and crash the party.

Eventually, Nash led them onto the porch to meet her.

The men straightened as they approached, looking immensely more serious and somber than they had as they'd greeted their teammate.

"This is Lana Iona," Nash said. "She's the witness to Tuesday night's murder."

"Ms. Iona," the men said in near unison.

Nash lifted a finger to the gray-haired man standing nearest him. "Victor Case."

He moved his pointer to the next, younger, shorter man. "James Friend."

Then the final team member, a ginger with dark-framed glasses. "Craig Lester."

Lana lifted a hand in greeting. "Nice to meet you."

The men wore khakis with button-shirts and ties.

Victor, the apparent oldest of the team, extended his hand to Lana for a shake. "I hear you're a chef."

Lana accepted the greeting with a smile. "I am."

"My wife and her sisters own a bakery in Louisville," he said. "They make a mean muffin."

The team chuckled, and Lana's smile grew.

"I love muffins," she said. "I hope to open a café one day." Her mouth pinched at the thought. She also hoped to survive long enough to see the dream come true.

Something shifted in her at the thought of becoming another of Mac Bane's victims, and she shuddered. There was so much more she wanted to see and do. Thirty years on this earth wasn't enough, and she was ready to fight for as many more as she could get. When this was over, she'd start making the most of her days.

Victor pulled a pink-and-white business card from his wallet and offered it to her. "If you ever have any questions about getting started, call my Maria. She loves to talk shop, and she's so proud."

"Rightfully," Lana said, taking the card with resolve. "You can tell her to expect my call."

Lana led the group inside and offered them coffee, then moved to the couch, where she could listen while they settled in.

Nash gave a verbal recap of the situation so far, condensing a couple days of extreme horror into a few manageable chunks. The other men responded with rapid-fire questions about everything from the processing of local crime scenes to small businesses in the town.

When the coffee was gone and the case fully rehashed, the men began to loosen their ties and kick back.

"I still can't believe you lived in this town before you came to Louisville," the man called Craig said. "After the military, right?"

Nash's gaze slid to Lana, and she averted her gaze.

"Four years," Nash said. "It's a great town, and I've got a lot of family here."

Craig nodded. "I recall hearing a few things about those years."

Victor chuckled. "Haven't we all? Will you stick around when we're finished?" he asked. "Maybe look someone up?"

The third team member, James, frowned. "No time. We have another case. Besides, don't give him any ideas."

Lana looked to Nash whose scowl had reached a new extreme.

"Let's focus on the case," Nash said. "We can talk about what happens next after we get Bane."

Craig's head tilted slightly, and he homed in on Lana, seeming to really see her for the first time. "How long have you lived in Great Falls, Ms. Iona?"

Her traitorous gaze slid to Nash before returning to Craig. "All my life."

The team traded looks.

Nash stiffened, and Victor noticed. His resulting expression became deeply curious. "Did the two of you know one another?" Victor asked Lana. "Before all this?"

Lana considered lying or attempting to sidestep the question, but she doubted the band of men before her missed much. They evaluated lies and read between the lines for a living. Even her lengthy pause had probably given away too much. "Yes."

Craig's eyes danced with curious delight. "So you know the woman he talks about anytime he's had more than two beers."

Nash pinched the bridge of his nose. "I'm sorry, Lana," he said flatly. "We're not usually so unprofessional when we're on duty."

Craig's look grew slightly strained, but he didn't relent. "I didn't mean to overstep. I just thought that since you knew her…" He pursed his lips. "And it's such a small town. Ms. Iona might want to help. Who doesn't enjoy a good love story?"

"You can call me Lana," Lana corrected, her mind

racing as Craig spoke. She absorbed the communal nods from Nash's other team members.

Did he say *love story*? Were they talking about her? Did Nash talk to them...about her?

"Lana," Craig repeated. His lips parted, and his attention darted to Nash.

The other men looked to him as well.

Nash exhaled. "We should probably discuss the possibility of a move," he said. "We have access to a mountaintop cabin my cousins are affectionately calling Old Smokey. It's just outside town, mostly off the grid and away from prying eyes. The general remoteness will come with perks and downfalls. Cell and Wi-Fi access are spotty, but we'll be better able to keep Lana out of sight there."

Victor cleared his throat and nodded, falling back into law-officer mode with visible effort. "Have you seen the place? Walked the perimeter?"

"No, but I trust Cruz and Derek," Nash said. "I have no reservations."

Victor nudged Craig. "Why don't you and I head over there, check it out, take some photos then regroup here with the team? We can talk through security and escape plans when we get back."

James pulled off his tie. "Give me a minute to change, and I'll come along. I'd like to see the place in person."

Nash nodded, and the team scattered. They retrieved their things from the SUV and traded their dress clothes for jeans, T-shirts and tennis shoes. They almost looked as if they belonged when they walked out the door.

Nash followed, passing Old Smokey's key to Victor, then pausing to text the GPS coordinates to the group.

Lana watched from the window, heart rate rising as Nash made his way back onto the porch. She met him at the threshold. "What do you say about me after two beers?" she asked, her voice nearly too breathless to be heard.

Nash raised his hands to her hips and tipped his head closer to hers. "That I lost a girl who meant the world to me. I messed up, and she moved on."

NASH FROZE, SHOCKED by the ease at which he'd reached for her and that the words had come without struggle.

"You tell the team about me," she clarified, without stepping away from his touch.

Nash spread his fingers against her sides, wanting to touch more of her, aching to reel her in closer. And she took a step forward in response. "I tell them I lost the only woman I've ever loved," he said, too rapt by her acceptance and that little step she'd taken in his direction to worry about scaring her away.

Her cheeks flushed with pleasure. A smile tugged her perfect pink lips. "You tell them you loved me?"

His pulse raced, and his muscles tensed. He

steeled himself for her reaction to the truth, because whatever she did or said next, he owed her at least that much. His fingers curled, aching to draw her nearer, to hold her in place and apologize if she didn't like his answer. "I tell them I love you. That I've been in love with you for twelve years."

Behind him, the team's SUV started, and the doors thumped shut.

Lana frowned, confusion piling on her brow. "You never came back," she said. "You never called."

"I came back once," he said, stomach clenching, regret rising. "About six months after I'd settled in to my new role as a Marshal. I felt like myself again. I was in a role where I excelled, doing something that felt good. I finally saw through the fog of depression that had taken hold before I left Great Falls. I understood I'd been pulling away from you and curling in on myself, but I hadn't been able to see that while I was in the middle of doing it. I realized all the mistakes I'd made with you and why. I thought I could explain myself and beg your forgiveness."

Lana's gaze shifted, and he could practically see her doing the mental math. Then her mouth formed a small o.

"I called to tell you I was in town, and a man answered your phone," he said, feeling the mix of anger and sadness as if he was back in that moment all over again. "I didn't give my name because he told me you were in the shower."

Lana closed her eyes, and when she reopened them, the pain he saw there was fresh.

"I'm not complaining," he said quickly, wholly gutted by the way his actions had changed everything about their futures. "We'd been over for months, and I had no right to think I could make a single phone call, or show up unannounced with a ring and an apology, and magically erase the hurt I'd caused you."

Lana set her palms against his chest. "His name was Thomas," she said. "I thought moving on was the best way to heal, so I accepted his invitation for coffee. We dated three months. He adored me. I thought he was nice."

Nash lifted his hands from her hips. "I don't need to know this. You don't owe me anything."

She curled her fingers in the material of his shirt. "He was nice," she repeated, "but he wasn't you."

Nash wet his lips, glancing at her hands on him and heating at the sight. Her nearness sent a wave of heat through his core, and he nearly vibrated with the need to know how her story would end. "What happened?"

"I realized he was in love with me, and I let him go. I was still in love with you."

A groan of deeply selfish satisfaction rumbled in Nash's core as he curved his arms around her back and pulled her against him. "I've never deserved you."

"Lies," she said, a small, proud smile forming on

her lips. "I saw you, Nash Winchester," she said. "I saw you then, and I see you now. And the man I see deserves the world."

Then she rose onto her toes and kissed him.

Chapter Eighteen

Lana skimmed her palms over Nash's shoulders and buried her fingers in the soft hair at the back of his head. She met his lips with a gentle sigh. The kiss was chaste and tentative as she waited to see if he wanted her too.

His body tensed, then animated with her kiss. The stoic, on-guard lawman, relaxed into her touch, meeting her sigh with a groan.

He kissed her back, sweetly, then with purpose.

She gasped as his lips parted, inviting her in.

Their mouths fell easily into a familiar rhythm. The slow, sexy dance she'd dreamed of more often than she'd ever admit.

He ended the kiss far too soon and set his forehead against hers with a chuckle. "We should probably take this inside."

Lana nodded, mesmerized as he brushed a thumb over his smiling, kiss swollen lips.

Cheering arose from the driveway.

His team hadn't left.

"Very professional," he muttered, waving a hand overhead as he ushered her inside.

Lana laughed as she stumbled into the foyer, steadied by Nash's strong arms.

He stilled suddenly, then looked over his shoulder at the retreating SUV. "Wait a minute," he said, turning back to her with a raised pointer finger. "Come on." He burst onto the porch and hurried down the steps, swinging both arms overhead, urging his team to come back.

Lana followed, unsure what was happening. Her lips still tingled from his kiss. Her mind was halfway to the bedroom.

Nash grabbed her hand when the SUV parked once more and led her to the vehicle, its windows already powering down.

The team wore matching cat-that-ate-the-canary expressions.

Her cheeks heated, but she kept her mouth closed, curious about what Nash would say next.

"I have an idea," he said, setting his free palm on the passenger door's open window frame. "We're considering a move to the mountain because we think it's a matter of time before Bane and his men find us here, but what if we let them find you?"

Nash looked at Lana, then back to his now gawking team. "If Old Smokey checks out, I think you guys should stay here," he said. "Let them find you. Leave your SUV out front. They shot mine, so they'll recognize yours and think they've found their target. Meanwhile, you'll be expecting them and can make the arrests. Even if Bane isn't one of the men who come, you can press the ones who do come for information on his location. Meanwhile, I'll take Lana onto the mountain. Derek and Cruz have already volunteered to keep watch. They're the only two people, other than us, who know we've even discussed relocating."

Butterflies took flight in Lana's middle at the thought of being alone with Nash. The kiss had left her body heated with promises of impossibly better things to come. Unfortunately, the thrill was dulled by fear for the men before her. She wasn't sure she'd emotionally survive seeing another life taken by Mac Bane.

Craig nodded slowly, seeming to consider the words a moment before a smile bloomed across his face. "I like it. We can set up an ambush and wait."

James rubbed his chin. "I do enjoy a good ambush. We can make a show of ordering food in town. Park on the busiest street, let folks spot our ride. Bane's men will think they found us because they're so clever."

Victor's gaze clung to Lana. "Don't worry about us," he said, clearly reading her mind. "Bane is clever. It's the reason he's a fugitive instead of incarcerated, but we're not too bad at what we do. We'll be just fine." Victor shifted his gaze to Nash. "Are you sure these PIs are up to the task you're describing?"

Nash released Lana's hand, in favor of sliding an

arm around her back and drawing her close. "Absolutely." One of his cheeks ticked up in a slow, crooked smile. "What do you think?" he asked her. "Feel like a trip to the mountains?"

She returned Victor's caring stare. "If you think it's safe for us there, I'm in."

"We'll let you know soon," he said.

The SUV's windows powered up, and the vehicle motored away.

Lana sent up silent prayers for everyone's safety, then she went inside to pack her things.

Two HOURS LATER, Nash held Lana's hand as he navigated the narrow, winding road away from town. Homes and farms fell away as the miles between them and his team increased. Groves of trees erupted in the place of rolling fields and meadows. Wildlife took the place of traffic and livestock. Eventually, the world darkened as mountains and forests rose on each side.

He checked his rearview mirror, then Lana's expression on repeat, making sure they weren't followed and that Lana was doing okay.

She'd kissed him like she meant it at the safe house, and his entire future had shifted as a result.

He couldn't leave her again, and he wasn't sure how to break the news to her or if she wanted to hear it. He only knew he had to stay. There was too much lost time to make up for already. There had to be a way to make things work between them.

He'd only dared hope for an opportunity to clear the air when he saw her. He'd wanted a chance to speak his peace and to leave her with the knowledge he hadn't meant to hurt her. Maybe to tell her how much he regretted his choices. He'd never dreamed she could still care for him too. And that changed everything.

He mentally tallied his accumulation of vacation and sick days. How long could he stay before he had to go back to work? What were the odds she'd return with him to Louisville? How long would it take to finally put Mac Bane behind bars?

Nash had everything to lose now, and every moment felt fragile and fleeting.

He eased his foot onto the brake pedal as a glint of sunlight off a windshield up ahead caught his eye. His muscles tensed, and his hand reached for his phone on instinct.

Derek stepped into view from behind the hood of an apparently broken-down car. He cast a disinterested look in their direction, then wiped his hands on a rag and went back to pretending not to know them.

"I guess our lookout man beat us here," Nash said, rolling his shoulders to release the tension.

"This is going to work, isn't it?" Lana asked.

The hope in her voice reached all the way to his heart. "That's the plan," he said, unsure if she meant the plan they'd set with his team or the two of them together. Either way, his answer was yes. He raised their joined hands to his lips and kissed her fingers.

A moment later, the GPS announced that they'd arrived.

Nash turned the pickup onto a weed-covered, deeply rutted dirt road.

No Trespassing signs were nailed to trees on either side as they rocked slowly up the mountainside. The midsize truck seemed like a giant on the narrow, untended road.

"This is steep," Lana said, staring through the windshield at the sharp precipice on his side.

"Feeling safer yet?" he joked, sounding significantly more at ease than was accurate.

She laughed nervously and pressed her back to the seat. "Unless Bane has a team of mountain goats, I can't imagine anyone coming for us up here."

Nash hoped she was right.

The small wooden cabin came into view a moment later, situated on a flat expanse of grass and surrounded by towering trees.

He parked the truck along the far side of the structure, hiding it as much as possible from anyone arriving by the same path.

Lana climbed out and stretched before making a slow arc around the cabin in exploration.

Nash checked his cell phone for service. Two small bars appeared, then vanished routinely, taking longer to return as he drew farther from the cabin's front porch. The larger bars, which usually signified a strong connection, never made an appearance.

"Is this for us?" Lana asked, climbing the small

flight of rough-hewn porch steps to Old Smokey's front door.

"Wait!" Nash darted in her direction, imagining everything from another threat to a bomb awaiting them.

She turned upon his arrival and handed him a long-range walkie-talkie.

Nash accepted the device with a sigh of relief.

White noise broke the silence, causing Lana to jump as he powered the device on. She giggled while Nash adjusted the volume.

"Breaker one-nine," Derek's voice announced. "This is Cowboy looking for my buddy Bat Girl."

Lana laughed again and set her hand on Nash's tender ribs. "I'm really sorry about that," she whispered.

Nash shook his head and depressed the walkie-talkie's button. He struggled not to flinch at the reminder of how effectively Lana had swung a make-shift bat at his middle. "We hear you, Cowboy. Is this a private channel?"

"Yep. How do you like Old Smokey?"

Lana leaned toward the device as Nash depressed the button once more. "It's perfect. Thank you."

"Don't mention it," he said. "Cruz and I are taking shifts down here. Make yourselves at home, and I'll call back if I hear anything worth telling."

"Appreciate it," Nash said, then passed the device to Lana. "This ought to be fun."

He collected their things from the truck and let them into the cabin with the key Derek had provided. A set of switches on the wall illuminated a lamp in the living room and an overhead fixture in the kitchen. Windows on three walls of the former showcased the forest. The small eat-in kitchen overlooked the living space, and a hallway began where the cabinets ended.

Lana made a loop through the space, admiring the views and looking more at ease than he'd seen her in days. He hoped their physical reconnection was at least a small part of the reason.

The walkie-talkie croaked again as Nash carried their bags into the first bedroom. The twin beds seemed incredibly far apart.

"Bat Girl and company," Derek said. "You out there?"

Nash rolled his eyes at being reduced to *and company*. He supposed it was better than *Boy Wonder*.

Lana's footfalls came quickly to meet him in the hall. "We're here," she said.

"I just heard from Knox," Derek said. "The coast guard found Mitchell Edwards's boat abandoned on the river. Edwards was not onboard."

Nash pulled Lana in close, her brokenhearted expression sending an ache through his chest and piling panic in his core. If Bane had gotten to Edwards, there was only one person left on his list.

Lana.

Chapter Nineteen

Nash held Lana's hand as she spoke to her parents once more. She'd found a place near the windows where reception was strongest and decided to call them before they called her. He stroked the hair from her shoulders, rubbed her back and smiled as she laughed at something her parents said. Being with her felt right, despite all the very wrong things going on in their lives. And he knew he'd never be happy without her.

He'd manage, if she sent him away, but he wouldn't be truly happy. Not like this.

She disconnected with a moan and collapsed against his chest. "I hate lying to my parents, but I don't know how to tell them about all of this without scaring them to death," she said. "I keep saying I'm fine, just very busy. I pretend not to be terrified, but I think they know I'm hiding things from them. I'm intentionally leaving out the truly terrible parts, and it feels icky. They say hello, by the way."

Nash smiled. "They don't hate me?"

"No," she said. "You left town for a job you'd always wanted. We weren't married. People break up. Plus, I was young, and you were my first love." She waved a hand in the air, briefly, then set it on his chest. "They probably assumed I'd find someone else."

He curled protective arms around her, hating the thought of her with someone else. Hating the time they'd lost. "You don't have to tell them more than makes you comfortable right now," Nash said. "You're buried in stress and managing the best you can. You're allowed to do that. If they had all the details, they'd only worry or show up in town looking for you. Worrying wouldn't change anything, and being here would put them in danger." He rested his chin on her head. "I'll explain everything to them when this is over. They can be angry with me, if they want."

The walkie-talkie grunted and gurgled on the coffee table. "Hey," Derek said.

Nash released Lana to answer. "We're here," he said. "Tell me you've got news."

"Maybe," Derek said, "A dark blue sedan has passed here twice in the last hour. I'm not convinced it's a reason for concern, but I wanted to pass it along. Cruz is on his way to extend the range of our lookout."

Lana folded her arms, face paling slightly at the news of a blue sedan. "Did it have Pennsylvania plates?" She looked to Nash while they waited for Derek's response.

"No."

She heaved a sigh, and Nash did his best not to follow suit. Signs of Mac Bane in this area would mean he already knew where they were.

She leaned toward the walkie-talkie, a frown wrinkling her brow. "Have you heard anything new about Mitchell Edwards?"

"Not much," Derek answered. "Knox says he's sending a dive team into the lake tomorrow. They're going to start where the boat was discovered, then fan out according to patterns in the current and see if Edwards turns up."

"You mean his body," Lana said, her voice thick with remorse.

Derek didn't respond.

AFTER DINNER THE next night, Lana fidgeted at Nash's side while he dialed Knox for an update. He set the phone on the small kitchen table and rested a hand over hers, probably attempting to infuse her with his calm.

It wasn't working. Too much time had passed without any new information. The isolation of a mountaintop cabin was starting to sink in. She was restless with worry, and Nash had spent the night pacing the perimeter, certain if he dared let his guard down, the cabin would be breached. Not exactly the evening she'd had in mind.

"Hey," Knox answered. "How's Old Smokey?"

"Good," Nash answered. "What's new with the case?"

The sound of shuffling papers rose from Knox's end of the line. "I'm still waiting for a full report on Edwards's boat," he said. "Deputies are cataloging the vessel's contents and expect to have that report tomorrow. The dive team came up empty. No signs of Edwards. And I just dispatched a unit to look into the car Derek saw twice on the main road through the mountains."

Lana nodded, though Knox couldn't see her. "The car didn't have Pennsylvania plates, like Bane's car had, so that's a small mark in our favor."

"It's easy enough to swap plates," Knox said. "Which is why I want you two to stay put. Derek told me about your little wilderness walk yesterday. If things go south and we need to do a fast extraction, you have to be where we expect you."

"We're in for the night," Nash said, rubbing Lana's back and offering a supportive look.

He'd agreed to take a short walk with her before bed last night. She'd needed the clear air and exercise. They hadn't gone far, but that wasn't the point. Just being able to leave the confines of Old Smokey, even for a few minutes, went a long way to making her feel at ease.

"Good," Knox said. "I've got another call, but I'll forward the photos from the boat and any other information. I have techs still working on the laptop."

Nash disconnected, and the text messages began to arrive. Images of stacks upon stacks of poker chips, playing cards, green felts and a thick notebook of hastily scrawled names and numbers appeared.

Nash rubbed his forehead. "Looks like a very serious boys' night," he said, replaying Lana's words from their time at the sheriff's department.

Tim and Mitchell loved to play cards, but there were enough supplies in the photos to host a casino night.

"I'm going to forward all this to the team, then give them a call," Nash said.

Lana watched as he attached each photo to an email, mind boggled by the sheer amount of materials. "There were a lot of names in that book," she said.

How many of those names would she recognize if she had a closer look? How many other people in her town were secretly involved with a fugitive?

Nash rose to collect two bottles of water from the refrigerator and brought them with him to the table, offering one to Lana. "This is all good news," he told her. "Evidence is good, however we can get it. Something on that boat will lead us to Bane or to someone who will tell us where to find him."

Lana sipped from her bottle, letting the cool liquid reduce the heat of unease and panic in her core.

Nash's phone rang, and Victor's face appeared on the screen.

"You're on Speaker," Nash said by way of greeting. He set the phone between them and returned to his seat.

"The photos you sent suggest someone was holding high-stakes poker nights on the boat," Victor said. "Lots of chips and big numbers in that notebook. The names seemed to be in code."

Nash folded his hands on the tabletop. "Could Mitchell Edwards and Tim Williams be the ones with the illegal-gambling operation? Not Bane?"

Victor grunted. "It would make a good side hustle for a restaurant manager and an accountant."

Lana covered her mouth as the pieces began to paint a new picture. "They could've been doing this long before Bane came to town," she said. "A small-scale operation to pad their bottom line."

"Maybe," Victor said. "If so, Mac Bane wouldn't have tolerated competition once he got here."

"Could he have brought them in with him?" Lana asked. "If they already had connections to local gamblers, they would've been valuable to him."

"Or," Victor interjected, "these two might've been gambling at Bane's newly established enterprise, then decided to offer the big spenders exclusive game nights on the boat. High rollers only."

"Poaching the whales straight out of Bane's hand," Nash said, rubbing his jawline. "Not a good idea. Bane would've seen that as betrayal and wanted retribution. He would've had to make an example of them, before anyone else got the same idea."

Lana's heart rate climbed. "Tim apologized that night," she said. "Bane said Tim overstepped."

Nash reached for her hand. "I'd like a better look at that notebook."

"Craig is headed to the station to take pictures of each page," Victor said. "We'll send them your way when we have them."

"Sounds good," Nash said. "Keep your eyes out while Craig's gone. You don't have a getaway vehicle now."

"We've got plenty of cameras," Victor said. "And your cousin Cruz is pretending to have car trouble at the end of the block."

Lana smiled, warmed by the knowledge everyone was looking out for everyone else and she was going to be okay.

If she could get Nash to relax a little, their night would only get better.

LANA PUT A kettle on the stove for herbal tea after the sun went down. She'd had enough coffee to keep her awake until Christmas, and her hands had begun to shake as a result.

The storm that seemed to be brewing for days finally hit at dusk, covering the mountaintop in a blanket of inky darkness. Rain pattered on Old Smokey's roof and swiveled in tiny rivers over the windows. Wind bent the trees all around them, whistling through the mountains and pushing clouds across the night sky.

Nash waved as he came into view outside the living-room windows, the soft glow of his phone screen illuminating his face. He'd walked the perimeter hourly instead of continuously, and she considered it a step in the right direction.

The cabin door opened, and he stepped inside, securing the lock behind him. "All clear," he said, setting his phone on the counter. He peeled off the hat and windbreaker he'd worn on his rounds and left both on a chair near the door.

His gaze caught on her, and a slow wolfish grin spread across his handsome face, as if she was indecent instead of dressed in an oversize T-shirt.

The night was hot, and she'd begun to sweat since her last shower, so she'd opted for her favorite sleep shirt in lieu of the T-shirt and yoga pants she'd been wearing all day.

She squeezed her thighs together as she rose onto her toes, opening a cabinet door in search of cups and saucers. "Tea?"

"Please," he said, scanning her lazily, from her messily pinned-up hair to her bare toes. He let his gaze linger on her most sensitive places in between.

Lana stifled a smile and turned to the cabinet. "I can make more coffee if you want. I'm hoping the tea will help me calm down."

"I can help you calm down," Nash offered, a teasing smile in his voice. He moved into her personal space and pressed his chest against her back pinning her to the countertop.

She shivered at the glide of his body against hers, and it took a long moment for her to realize he was opening the cabinet door above her head.

He retrieved a bottle of Kentucky bourbon, then stepped away with a grin. "This goes great with tea," he said. "And it's excellent at helping folks unwind."

She laughed at the sight of the bottle. "Derek's?" she guessed.

"Yep." Nash grinned. "He told me about it during my latest perimeter check." His eyes flickered to the walkie-talkie on the counter as he removed the bottle's cap and added a dash of whiskey to each of the empty cups.

Lana lifted the drink closest to her and tossed the whiskey back with a gulp. Her eyes and throat burned briefly, and she knew the benefits were close behind.

Nash laughed. "You still shoot whiskey."

"I do." Sharing a shot or two with the restaurant staff after a chaotic night of work had become the tradition that kept them running like a team. Plus, Lana liked whiskey.

She hopped onto the counter and crossed her legs at the ankles, waiting patiently for the kettle to sing.

"Another?" he asked, wiggling the bottle between them, then adding a bit more to her empty cup.

Her gaze dropped to his mouth, and he set the bottle aside. "One's enough," she said. "I'm feeling less anxious already."

His brows tented, and he pressed one of his broad

palms beside each of her bare thighs. "Is that right? How, exactly, are you feeling?"

"Better all the time," she whispered against his stubbled cheek.

When he didn't make a move to leave, she gripped his hands and raised them to her body, pressing them where she needed his touch most.

Nash swore, and his mouth crashed over hers. His broad, skilled hands were everywhere she wanted them, tracing and caressing the curves of her breasts through her shirt, while he kissed her senseless. When she was sure she'd gone boneless from his touch, he curled warm palms over her knees, and heat shot through her core. He slid hot calloused palms along the tender flesh of her thighs, parting them to make room for his hips, then grazing the bare skin of her sides beneath the shirt.

Lana's ankles locked behind his waist, pulling him closer and needing more.

He moaned into her mouth, and her head fell back in pleasure. No one had ever made her feel this good. Nash had been her first love. Her first everything. And her perfect match in every way.

"Lana," he whispered, gripping her hips as she pressed needily against him.

The strain in his tone was evident, his self-control reaching its limit as he lowered his gaze to her chest. She watched his thumbs trace paths over the taut peaks of her nipples, the nightshirt hiked high to expose it all.

"Nash," she said, turning off the burner and removing her shirt in answer to his unspoken question. And leaving herself bare before him. "I want you too," she whispered.

She nipped at his lips and urged his hands back to their work. "Touch me. Please."

His pupils dilated, and he pulled her off the countertop with one swift flex of his arms.

Lana squeaked her thrilled response.

And Nash carried her straight to the bedroom.

Chapter Twenty

Lana opened her eyes hours later, peaceful and satiated. She turned slowly in the warm cocoon of sheets, a mental montage of the previous night's lovemaking still dancing in her heart. She squinted at the empty space beside her, where Nash had pushed the second bed against the first so they could sleep comfortably together. She ran her palm over the cool material.

She rose to her elbows, listening closely to the silent cabin. Her mind raced over a host of possibilities from bad to awful. Had Nash gone to check on a noise and been hurt by the fugitive hunting her? Had he regretted what they'd done last night and slipped away so he wouldn't give her false hope for something more?

She wasn't sure she could live with either scenario.

The front door opened and closed, bringing with it the low rumble of Nash's voice. She swung her legs over the bed's edge, then stilled. The creak of floorboards suggested he was walking as he talked, but the cabin was small, and pacing was never a good sign.

She dressed quickly and raked a brush through her hair, then checked her face in the reflection of the bedroom window. The peace she'd woken with was gone, replaced by fear for her heart and her life. So she squared her shoulders and padded down the short hall to the kitchen, prepared to face whatever was happening now.

Nash stood at the countertop, filling the old coffee maker with water. The walkie-talkie rested on the counter where she'd sat the night before. She closed her eyes against the flash of memory. She'd been thoroughly worshipped and devoured by the gorgeous, gentle-hearted protector before her. A man who'd told her he loved her in the afternoon, then made love to her like he'd meant it last night.

"Hey," he said.

"Hey." An unexpected rush of nerves anchored her in place. Bane hadn't gotten to Nash while she slept, but what if her other fear had come true?

He looked her over, a strange tension buzzing in the air. She'd unknowingly dressed like him. Both in heather-gray T-shirts, bare feet and jeans. His shirt had *ARMY* printed across the chest in large block letters and tiny holes along the hem. Her shirt was plain with a little pocket.

He turned briefly away and adjusted a nob on the oven. "You caught me," he said. "There are casseroles in the freezer, and I'm making you breakfast." An impish grin softened his features when he looked at her again. He appeared younger and less dangerous in moments like those.

She appreciated both sides of him equally.

But the physical distance between them was slowly becoming a moat.

Nash opened the oven door and slid a baking dish covered with foil inside. He narrowed his eyes at her when he finished. "What's wrong?"

She shook her head. "It's just time for coffee." Maybe a mug or ten would help her shake the fog and get refocused. It wasn't time to worry about whether or not she'd made a bad decision last night or if Nash had meant the things he'd said. Now was the time to worry about whether or not they'd live long enough to have a future, together or apart.

Nash's head tilted slightly, possibly reading her mind. He watched closely as she placed her mug beneath the drip, gathering the dark drops as they were created. "Talk to me."

She struggled for several long beats, choosing her words carefully before replacing the pot. "I'm still waking up," she said, finally. She took a ginger sip from her mug and met his eyes. "How about you? You seem—" she paused again, not wanting to open a can of worms but needing to voice the concern "—distant."

He sagged against the counter and rubbed an open palm over the top of his head. "I've never been much of an actor with you."

The words were a punch to the gut, but she edged her chin up and forced a small, confident smile. "You don't have to act with me."

"Okay." He met her gaze with a deeply remorseful expression. "Then we need to talk."

Ice trickled over her skin, and she set the mug aside, certain she'd drop it otherwise. "Just say it," she said. "Whatever you want to say, just go on. I can handle the truth." She was sure the last statement was an enormous lie but didn't want him to hold back on her account. It was always better to have the facts. She tented her brows in question.

Nash reached for her hand. "Let's sit."

She let him lead her to the small sofa in the living area, before the endless windows. He waited for her to take a seat, then he crouched on the floor before her, bringing their eyes nearly level. He cupped her cheeks gently in his hands, as if she was made of glass.

Her stomach rocked, and heat climbed her chest, throat and face, certain she didn't want to hear whatever came next. Positive he was attempting to let her down easily. He'd changed his mind about her again.

Nash's thumbs caressed the sensitive skin along her jaw. "Knox gave Derek some bad news."

Her breath caught, and her mind stalled. This was about the case? "What happened? Is it bad news about Bane?" she asked, unreasonably relieved Nash wasn't trying to tell her they'd made a mistake last night.

He nodded once, tight and short. "Yes."

She released a long, slow breath, and he frowned.

A moment later, his eyes widened as recognition of her thoughts seemed to dawn. He pulled her to the edge of the couch and pressed his forehead to hers. "We're good," he promised. "And we're going to get through this."

She nodded, and he pulled away, gripping her hands in his.

"The bad news," he said, "is that the media somehow got wind of Mac Bane's presence in Great Falls, and they've labeled you a missing person. Your face is everywhere. Online and in the morning paper. You name it."

Lana worked the information over, trying to see what about these statements had turned Nash's healthy, sun-tanned skin so pale and ashen. She'd need to call her parents. Leave a message if necessary. So they'd know she was okay. "What does that mean to us?" she asked, finally. She was hidden, so she was safe. Wasn't she? "Be specific," she added.

A mix of fire and determination curled like smoke in the depths of Nash's blue eyes. "It means the town, the county and half the state is looking for you."

"Looking for me," she repeated.

"Yes." Nash dropped his hands to hers and squeezed.

There was more he hadn't said.

"Go on," she encouraged. "Take your time, but tell me."

He wet his lips. His expression went flat and hard.

"Marshals back in Louisville noted a significant migration of Bane's known associates last night. Sources have suggested they were dispatched for a mission."

The invisible weight on his shoulders seemed to spread onto hers, and she fought the urge to topple. "They're coming for me," she whispered.

Nash inclined his head, and her heart split down the center.

Chapter Twenty-One

Lana chewed the tender skin along her thumbnail, a nervous habit she'd broken as a teen but found comfort in now. She'd left a calm, if vague, message for her folks and Knox's number, so they could check in with him for details as needed. Lana was scared, but her parents were probably going to lose their minds. Rightfully.

A criminal army was on their way to find her, and the entire town would be eager to help, assuming she was truly lost and not in hiding.

Nash hovered over his phone screen, where he and several members of their makeshift task force had gathered on a web call to trade information.

She stayed close enough to listen in, but far enough away to remain off-screen. They didn't need to see her shake and sweat. Plus, fear-vomiting in front of strangers was on her never-do list, and that was one small thing she could control.

She shuffled onto the porch, leaving the door open behind her, and peered down the narrow, rutted road they'd arrived on. She imagined Derek keeping watch below, and she owed him everything for his dedication.

Her heart and head jerked at every cracking branch and crunch of leaves, certain she'd find a gunman at the site of the sound. She gasped softly at the stirring of birds, squirrels and occasional deer. Her heart suddenly went out to all the wildlife. She'd grown up surrounded by hunters, without giving the concept much thought. Today, however, she identified with the unarmed, defenseless prey.

If she survived this, she'd revisit the kinds of meat she purchased for her kitchen. Being shoved ten rungs down the food chain was an instant perspective-shifter.

Nash stepped through the doorway. "How are you doing?"

She smiled, and her arms tightened their grip around her center. "Terrible."

"Come here." He pulled her close and enveloped her with his embrace, then set his cheek against the top of her head.

"Thank you," she whispered.

"Anytime," he offered. "Maybe you should come and sit down."

Slowly, she peeled away. Her legs were weak and numb. Her head too fuzzy with fear to argue. "Yeah."

He motioned to a pair of chairs they'd carried outside earlier, after the news had been delivered, and she was desperate for the cool morning air. She lowered into one. Nash took the other.

"How'd the call go?" she asked.

"Good," he said. "Bane's guys scattered as they moved, so the Marshals couldn't adequately track them all, but we're reasonably certain they're headed this way. It's the closest we've been to catching him, and we've never had an eyewitness willing to talk. We've been building cases against him that will put him away a long time, but Tim's murder conviction will remove his possibility of ever getting out. And we won't let him escape again."

Lana kneaded her hands on her lap. "I guess it's good that we moved to the mountain before they got here or told the world to look for me."

"Agreed," Nash said. "Knox and the rest of the county deputies are chasing every lead in search of Bane or anyone who can lead them to him. Eventually, they'll find a weak link, and he or she will give up the information we need in exchange for leniency or protection."

Lana chewed her thumbnail. "Have they gotten many leads?"

"A few," he said, "but remember, they only need one good one."

The sound of an incoming web call drew Nash back inside.

"Hey." Knox's voice echoed through the speaker, followed by similar greetings from Derek and Cruz. "I'm stopping at Rizzo's to talk to a delivery guy about a lead. I thought I could pick up pizzas or sandwiches for y'all if you want anything. I know Aunt Rosa's frozen casseroles can get tiresome, especially for a chef. And I'm not even sure what you're eating out there, Derek. When was the last time you went home or got some sleep?"

Lana rose to join the call. This time, it was her friends on the line. Faces she liked to see. And the topic, for once, wasn't her imminent abduction or death. She moved in close to Nash's side and waved at the screen.

The group paused their discussion of Rizzo's calzones versus double-crust pizzas to say hello.

"I'm in," Derek said, "but how are you getting food to Nash and Lana?"

Knox sucked his teeth, averting his gaze a minute. "I can deliver it to the family cabin," he suggested. "It's not more than a mile east. You guys can have dinner out when you're ready." He smiled. "Assuming things stay quiet on the crime front, of course."

Nash slid his arm around Lana and pulled her against his side. "I think we'll stick with what we've got here. Rizzo's is good, but Lana is better."

She smiled.

"How are things on the crime front?" Nash asked. "Is the lead you're following to Rizzo's a strong one?"

Knox shrugged. "The guy is young, but I've heard he's living a little larger than usual and too large for a pizza-delivery guy. It's not much, but it's what I have to pull on, so—"

"Derek?" Cruz said, interrupting. "What did the car you saw drive up and down the mountain yesterday look like?"

"Navy sedan," Derek said.

The men went silent and still.

Cruz tracked something off-camera with his gaze.

"Why?" Derek asked.

"Because this car," Cruz said, moving the camera to face the road, "has passed three times in eight minutes."

A compact sedan moved in Cruz's direction, and he took a still shot as the driver passed.

"Anyone recognize him?" Cruz asked. "Should I follow him? Or is he some dad dropping off and picking up kids from soccer?"

Nash stretched the still shot of the car and driver until it filled the screen. The curse that followed silenced his cousins once more. He swiped the image aside, a rush of energy bristling around him. "Cruz, that's Mark Dunfel. A marksman and a paid gun for hire. Stay away from him. Knox, get your people over there. Did you get a plate number?"

Lana stumbled back a step, listening as Nash delivered the orders.

"He's parking," Cruz said, changing the angle of the camera to show distant brake lights near the end of the street he guarded. The street the safe house stood at the end of. "Call your team," he told

Nash. "Tell them to watch the security cameras. He's coming."

"On it," Nash said, adding another number to the call.

"I don't see him," Cruz said, panning the camera across the distant lawns and empty street. "He went into all that damn shade and vanished."

A series of rhythmic dinging rose through the phone's speaker in unison.

"You getting those?" Derek asked.

"I am," Cruz said, the soft snick of a closing car door accompanying his words. "He took out the security system."

Derek cursed. "We pay for all the bells and whistles. Who can disarm an entire system like that? It's been thirty seconds."

Nash tapped nervous fingers beside the phone, waiting for his team to pick up. "Mark is a professional. He works with criminals way up the food chain. I had no idea he had ties to Bane."

Victor's face appeared on-screen. "Sorry, we were talking with the team back home about the migration," he said. "What's up?"

"Mark Dunfel is outside your home. He disarmed the—" Nash froze.

Victor's image had vanished.

"Cell blocker," Derek suggested. "What can you see, Cruz?"

"Where are those deputies?" Nash barked. "They need backup. Now!"

Gunfire erupted over the line.

Cruz cursed and began to run. Images of blurring grass and gravel raced beneath his phone.

Nash yelled for Cruz to stand down. For Knox to get himself in gear. And for his team, no longer connected to the call, to look out.

The screen went black as the shots grew louder and more sporadic, then a single shot reverberated through the speaker, loud enough to make Lana's ears ring.

Cruz vanished from the call.

Lana released a heart-wrenching cry.

"Cruz!" Knox screamed, the panic in his voice ripped straight through Lana, gutting her where she stood. Had he just watched his older brother die?

Slowly, the camera's view returned. Cruz's panting breaths came with an image of Mark on the ground. "He's dead," Cruz said. "I had to take the shot. The cell blocker trashed my signal, but I got that off. The Marshals have all been hit. We need ambulances."

"Already on it," Knox said, a quake to his usually stoic tone.

The distant wails of emergency vehicles were audible in seconds.

Cruz pounded a fist against the front wall, where the window had been broken by gunfire. "Shooter down. It's Cruz Winchester. I'm coming in for triage." He crunched over shards of broken glass to let himself in with his key.

Victor sat against one wall, a palm pressed to a large crimson stain on his side. "I'll be okay," he said. "Check on James and Craig."

Another series of beeps caused Derek to check his phone.

Cruz ignored the sounds as he moved into the next room to evaluate the other Marshals.

"Nash," Derek said, eyes wild as he returned his attention to the camera, "the security systems are going down at all our other properties."

"You're compromised," Knox said, already in his cruiser, on his way to the scene of the shooting.

"Nash," Derek said, "get Lana off the mountain."

NASH ENDED THE call and shoved the phone into his pocket. Training pushed his body into motion, but the weight of his love for Lana added a new and unfamiliar strain.

There wasn't time for hesitation or delay. There wasn't room for error.

"Lana?" he asked, catching her paralyzed gaze in his. "You're going to be okay, but we need to move."

She turned numbly for the door.

"Put on your shoes and grab your phone," he said, stuffing his feet into the boots he'd left waiting on the mat. "All our things can stay here until we're able to come back for them. The goal right now is to put as much distance as possible between us and this property. It's only a matter of time before Bane and his men realize it's owned by Derek and Cruz's umbrella company." If they didn't know already.

Lana moved stoically onto the porch, looking back for further instructions.

"Here we go," he said, taking her hand. "We can do this. Are you ready?"

Nash didn't wait for her response. Together, they launched onto the soggy ground and made a run for the waiting truck. He scanned the forest in broad sweeping arcs as they dove into their escape vehicle, and he shifted immediately into gear. A three-point turn later and they were headed back down the path that had brought them to the cabin only two nights before. This time, however, the narrow, rutted road was nearly washed away. "The storms," he muttered, evaluating the extent of the damage and their complete lack of alternative routes.

"Put on your seat belt," he said, casting a furtive glance at Lana. "And pray we don't slide over the mountain on our way back down."

Lana buckled up and clutched the safety belt across her chest.

Nash nudged the gas pedal and hoped there was still time to get to the main road before one of Bane's men found his way to them.

The truck's tires dug into the loosely packed mud and spun as the engine revved.

"Come on," Nash urged, gripping the steering wheel until his knuckles were white with effort.

The truck lurched forward, its wheels grabbing

traction, and a breath of relief whooshed from Nash's chest. He had one job now. Get Lana to safety. He wasn't going to fail.

The truck plowed on, sliding and bouncing over a barely there road, while Nash did his best to avoid the jagged cliff on one side.

Lana whimpered as the tires lost purchase again, and the back end swung wide.

"We're okay," Nash murmured like a mantra. "We're nearly halfway there now. We haven't heard more from Derek, and that's good news. It means the danger hasn't reached us yet."

The walkie-talkie barked to life in the cup holder.

Lana grabbed it before Nash could make the suggestion.

Derek's voice broke through the static. "Incoming," he announced, his voice a ragged whisper. "I don't know where you are, or what you're doing right now, but you need to get off that mountain. Avoid the direct path down. If they're here, it means they know exactly where to find Old Smokey."

"We're in the truck," Lana said. "We're halfway to you."

"Go back," Derek said. "My informant, playing lookout, says they're headed our way. Let's avoid a shoot-out and meet at the family cabin. Head east and stay high on the mountain."

"Yep," Nash agreed, gritting his teeth and shifting into Reverse.

Lana cast a disbelieving gaze his way. "We're going back?" she asked.

The truck's wheels sank into soft, muddy earth and spun. They weren't going anywhere in this vehicle.

"No," Lana said, exhaling the word.

"What?" Derek called, the sound of his car's engine increasing in the background.

"We're stuck," she explained. "The mud from the storm washed out the road."

"Then you go on foot," Derek said. "Move quickly."

Nash threw the shifter into Park and turned for her with as much resolve as he could muster. "We can make it to the other cabin. It's only a mile, and it's a big forest out there. We can hide among the trees until we get there, then Derek will pick us up."

Lana scanned the world outside her window, pale and afraid. "Okay," she whispered. She unbuckled her seat belt, grabbed the walkie-talkie and opened her door. "We're going," she told Derek. And she climbed down from the cab.

Nash met her at the tailgate in three long strides.

The first gunshot echoed across the mountain like a blast of thunder, and the truck's windshield exploded.

"Get down," Nash called, ducking as he grabbed Lana's hand.

She screamed. One arm covered her head. The other clung to Nash.

The next bullet sent a spray of bark into the air as it hit a tree only a few feet away.

"Run," he said, pulling her forward, then over the hillside into an avalanche of mud and leaves. They scrambled downward, falling and sliding.

Her hand was torn from his as they rolled. Every thump of the ground against his back and head sent reverberating pain through his body. He feared they'd roll off a cliff before they stopped or would collide with a tree along the way. They could die before they'd ever had a chance to hide.

The world blurred and spun around him as he worked his arms and legs, attempting to slow his progress and catch himself on something solid.

Eventually, they crashed onto a plateau.

His world was still spinning, the blasts of pain still occurring, when the gunshots began again.

Nash rolled onto his hands and knees, finding his balance and searching for the only thing that mattered. "Lana!"

A rustling drew his attention to a small pile of limbs and leaves at the plateau's edge.

"Nash," she said, an arm extending from the pile.

He scurried to her, staying low to the ground and dragging her with him to the nearest tree. "Are you okay?" he asked, pressing her back to the bark and examining the welts and bruises over her face, neck and arms. A trickle of blood rolled from her lips. A cut, he realized, not a sign of internal injuries.

"We have to keep moving," he said. "Can you do that?"

Lana nodded.

The shooter had the advantage of higher ground, which meant Nash needed to find a place they could hide.

He and Lana darted from tree to tree, selecting the broadest they could find, and making a steady path toward the family cabin. Nash watched during each short break, searching for signs of the shooter, a chance to pull his sidearm and finish this. Instead, there were only endless shadows and trees.

Yet, each time they ran, another bullet landed close enough to make Lana scream.

Nash pulled her in close and kissed her head while she caught her breath. She trembled in his arms, flinching at each new round of gunfire. But she never complained. And she never stopped.

"You can run," a deep male voice called from above, his words magnified by the natural acoustics of the mountains. "But you can't hide."

Nash imagined all the ways he would stop this stranger's reign of terror if he knew Lana could wait for him safely to return. But she needed him, and that was his priority.

"It's better for both of us if you just bring the girl out here," the booming voice continued. "We can settle up. Come to an agreement," he suggested. "My beef isn't with you, Marshal."

Nash scanned the forest, desperate for someplace to hide Lana while he found a way to stop the hunter. "Your beef isn't with her either," he bellowed back.

The rocky face of a cliff was visible several dozen

yards away. The run would be longer than any they'd made so far between trees. It would be risky, but the rocks would provide the cover Nash and Lana needed while they made a better plan.

And it would force the shooter to give up his position on higher ground.

Nash held Lana's eye contact when she looked to him for directions on what was next. He pointed to the rock face, and her eyes slid slowly shut. A moment later, they opened, and she nodded. He pressed a kiss to her forehead and lifted the fingers on his free hand, one by one.

One.

Two.

Three.

And they ran.

For one long moment, the sound of maniacal laughter rattled the world around them. Then the shots began. And a bullet ripped through Nash's thigh.

Chapter Twenty-Two

Lana pressed her back to the rough and jagged stones of the cliff face as it protruded from the mountain. Her heart hammered. Her throat and chest burned. But she was shielded from the shooter, and that was everything.

She blinked stinging eyes and urged her lungs to find more oxygen while she turned in the direction she'd come. Barely a heartbeat had passed since her arrival on the rocks, but instinct screamed up her spine. Something was wrong.

Nash was gone.

Every other time they'd run, he'd landed on her heels and held her close while they regrouped their thoughts and collected their breath. He'd pressed a kiss to her head or squeezed her hand in silent reassurance that he knew what he was doing, and they would be okay.

But where was he now? And when had he vanished?

Panic seized her already-constricted chest as she

searched the endless mountain for signs of him, visually retracing her path. Claws of understanding dug ragged trenches through her heart when he finally came into view.

Ten yards away, Nash lay on the forest floor, filthy and outlined in the aftermath of an avalanche of leaves. His face contorted in pain, but he was silent. Both hands gripped his left thigh. Blood soaked his pant leg and oozed between his fingers.

Nash had been shot.

Lana's ears rang, and her vision tunneled. Her protector was down, and they were still being hunted.

How could they survive this now?

"Nash," she called, begging him to look her way. Tears burned hot, thick trails across her cheeks. "Can you hear me?"

His grimace deepened, but he gave a small nod.

"Can you walk?"

He nodded once more, then attempted to rise.

Her heart expanded, infused with hope and possibility as silence gonged over the mountain. The shooter was there, but invisible. The danger was real and present. But Nash was getting up, and they would be okay.

She shook her hands out hard at the wrists, imagining she could shed her fear like an unwanted coat. Then she left it on the rocks at her feet.

Without making the conscious decision, Lana was in motion, racing to the place where Nash struggled onto his hands and one knee. His injured leg lay out-stretched behind him, as if immobile.

How would he keep moving along the mountain on one leg? How could they cover their tracks with him bleeding? Could they hide at the cliff and wait for the shooter to approach? Nash had been a mili-tary sharpshooter. He could surely hold the assailant off until help arrived.

Couldn't he?

How many rounds were in his clip?

Did he have more with him?

Nash collapsed before her with a grunt.

"Nash." She threw herself forward, sliding over the dirt and leaves to his side. "I'm here," she whis-pered. "I can help, but you have to get up." She latched on to him, pulling his torso up by an inch, willing him to do the rest.

Nash screamed, and she released him, falling back beneath his weight.

The deep roar of laughter echoed through the for-est once again. "Attaboy," he called. "Keep making noise so I can find you."

Lana bit her trembling lip, terrified but finding hope in the shooter's telling taunt. He'd lost track of them during the run. Whether Nash had been hit by a stray bullet or had kept going long enough af-terward to disappear among the trees, they now had time to make a plan.

They just couldn't do it in the open as they were.

Nash made a strangled, choking sound as he struggled against a pain she couldn't imagine.

She flattened herself on the ground at his side. "We have to move."

He shook his head against the earth. "I can't go any farther. I've lost too much blood." He worked to swallow, then speak once more. "Leave me. Complete the mission," he whispered. "Reach Derek. Help is on the way."

Lana pressed a palm to his cheek and forced him to meet her eyes. "On the way where?" she asked. "Do you hear sirens? Engines? Emergency responders? Because I don't. It's me and you, and I won't leave you here alone." She slapped the ground with one hand in punctuation, then rose to grip his arm and roll him onto his back.

He stifled another roar of pain.

She crouched at the top of his head and wound her arms beneath his, determination replacing every other thought and erasing her fear. "We were supposed to make a straight line from Old Smokey to your family's cabin, but we rolled down the hill, and we've been running. I don't have any idea how far off course we are or in which direction we've been going."

Nash's eyes closed, and his arms went limp.

Lana pressed her heels into the earth and began a slow retreat to the rocks. Nash's large body left a broad path in their wake. People in the next county, or maybe on the moon, could easily see the direction they'd gone. But she didn't have time or energy to spend covering it. And she couldn't risk exposing herself to get the job done. All she could do was hope and hide.

She forged on, sweating and straining. Dragging the body of the strongest man she knew, inch by inch over rough, uneven mountain terrain.

Sweat rolled over her brow and into her eyes, blinding and stinging her as she kept the slow, steady pace. Her arms, back and legs burned and protested the effort, while the air felt too thin to properly nourish her lungs. Panic was returning, the coat of fear taking shape once more.

"You can do this," she told herself, whispering aloud in case Nash could hear her too. "You can do anything. You are strong. You are smart. You are not a monster's prey."

And Nash will die if I don't keep moving.

Her heels met rock in the next pull, and tears of joy ran fresh and new. She arranged Nash on his back along the cliff face, adding handfuls of leaves and small stacks of stones to mask the color of his jeans. Then she pulled out her phone to check for service.

A single bar of Wi-Fi blinked unstably, and she nearly cried out with joy. She ran her fingers over the screen, searching for the nearest network, and she found it with a bark of shocked laughter.

Winchester_Country

Somehow, impossibly, and against all odds, they'd made it within Wi-Fi range of Nash's family cabin.

Sobs of relief burst uncontrollably from her core, and she buried her face in the crook of her arm to cover the sound. She settled her breathing and leaned over Nash once more. "We made it," she whispered, kissing his face and wiping sweat-dampened hair from his forehead. "We're here."

His eyes opened slowly, unfocused and seeking.

"I think your family's cabin is at the top of this hill, above this plateau and the rocks," she said. "I'm going to try to make it."

Nash's expression twisted with pain.

"I'm going to get help," she promised. "You're going to be okay."

He rocked his head slowly left to right. "I've lost too much blood."

Ice washed over her skin in a mind-numbing flood. She forced her eyes to the place where blood flowed dark and thick. The wound would take Nash's life if she let it. And she would not let it.

"Okay," she said. "I'm taking your belt for a tourniquet."

He took a steadying breath as she unfastened his belt and worked it slowly from the loops of his jeans.

She circled his thigh with the leather strap, arranging it above the injury and thanking her parents for the mandatory wilderness-survival lessons they'd forced her into as a child. Lessons she'd never believed she'd need. She pulled and prayed, then watched as his eyes shut and his pale face tipped away. "I love you," she whispered.

Then she started up the mountain.

Lana forced her body beyond the point of exertion, promising herself with each tortured step that everything would somehow be okay. Derek would meet her, and she would be okay. Emergency responders would reach Nash, and he would be okay. Deputies would find the shooter prowling over the mountain, and he would be arrested.

Things would be okay.

She stopped at the last of the massive trees broad enough to shield her, and she pressed her back against an oak to bolster her resolve. Below her, the rocky cliff protruded from the mountainside, and her heart was bleeding out at its base. Above her was the cabin where Derek had promised to meet them.

Around her was endless forest, where the shooter could be lying in wait.

Lana took small, careful sips of air, willing herself to be strong.

She scanned the forest again for signs of the shooter, then turned her phone over in her hands and texted Derek. She sent a rushed, typo-riddled rundown of her location and situation, then waited for instructions. For assurance he was there. Or for news of a changed plan.

But Derek didn't respond.

And the world was silent around her.

No singing birds or chattering squirrels. No distant wails of emergency vehicles on their way to save the day.

Just her shuddered breaths and the knowledge a gunman waited for her next move.

Chapter Twenty-Three

Lana watched the little bars on her cell phone blink in and out. She hit Send on her call to 9-1-1 for the tenth time, while she waited for Derek to answer her text.

The call refused to connect, and she knew she had to get closer to the cabin.

The clearing around the structure was eerily silent as she held her breath in wait. There weren't any vehicles in the driveway. Or signs anyone had been there in recent days.

What had happened to Derek?

And where were the first responders?

Lana cringed as a horrific thought came to mind. Could one of the many gunshots she'd heard while running with Nash have been aimed accurately at his cousin?

She shoved the dark idea aside, unable to bear the thought of anyone else being hurt today. She had to stay focused. And she had to move closer to the cabin.

With no other choice, and one more scan of the area, she stepped out from the trees.

The blinking bars on her phone screen doubled, then stabilized.

"Oh, thank goodness," she whispered and slammed her thumb against the Send button once more.

"This is 9-1-1," a tinny voice announced on the other end of the line. "What's your emergency?"

"Hello! This is Lana Iona. I'm at the Winchester family's cabin on Great Mountain Drive. I don't know the address. US Marshal Nash Winchester has been shot, and the shooter is still in the forest." Lana's voice cracked, and a painful wedge of emotion clogged her tightening throat. "Nash needs an ambulance," she added. "Please help us."

The quiet click of a gun's hammer being drawn ended her speech.

"Give me your phone," a low, gravelly voice instructed.

Lana recognized the sound immediately from the vicious taunts he'd called into the forest. And from the restaurant's roof. She hadn't realized while she'd been running, but she knew now.

Mac Bane was the shooter.

She shut her eyes and turned slowly toward him, lowering the phone.

"Good girl," he seethed, snatching the device from her palm. She hoped the 9-1-1 operator was still listening. And that she'd dispatched help.

A sickening crunch opened her eyes, and she watched, helplessly, as a black-booted foot stomped her phone into pieces.

Lana raised her gaze to the man's face and found it gut-wrenchingly familiar.

Bane stared down his nose at her with a victorious and satisfied sneer. His hair was dark and slick with sweat, pushed off his face in a style that reminded her of greasers in old movies. His black shirt and jeans supported the look.

"Why are you doing this?" she asked, struggling to speak past the swelling lump in her throat.

"I'm cleaning up loose ends," he said. "Sometimes when I want something done right, I have to do it myself." He snaked out an arm, and his fingers tightened on her wrist, yanking her close.

Lana whimpered and twisted, attempting to break free, but his viselike grip only tightened.

"You're a tough one," he said, "I'll give you that. Tougher than that Marshal and his idiot team of law enforcement."

Before Lana could speak or protest, Bane gave a powerful shove, and she collided with the ground. Pain shot through her hip and shoulder, sending bolts of light into her vision and making her ears ring once more. She cried out, and he raised his gun. "I love small towns," he said. "People climbed all over one another to tell me where you were, just because I asked. Someone even told me they saw you with Nash Winchester, a current US Marshal and your former boyfriend." He tipped his head toward the hill she'd just climbed. "I plan to have a talk with him next."

"Don't touch him," she warned, desperately scanning the ground for something she could use as a weapon. Sticks and rocks were plentiful, but all were just beyond her reach.

Bane raised his free palm in mock surrender. "I'm not planning to lay a finger on him," he said. "But I am going to finish unloading these bullets. One for him, and one for you." He directed the gun's barrel at her head.

She squeezed her eyes shut and extended her fingers, wondering if she could reach the nearest stick before Bane could squeeze the trigger.

The reverberating blast of a gunshot ripped a scream from her throat.

She rolled toward the sticks, waiting for pain that didn't come. Her eyes opened in shock.

Bane gripped his shoulder and stumbled, eyes wide and fighting for balance. A crimson stain unfurled beneath his palm.

Lana scanned her unharmed body, then the trees and driveway running alongside the cabin, searching without seeing the source of this man's shooter.

He raised his free, trembling hand once more. The gun wobbled in his weakened grip.

Lana wrapped her fingers around the largest stick in reach and rose, already swinging. The sturdy, fallen branch met Bane's leg with a crack, and he crashed to the ground with a shout. She dove for his gun and pointed it at his head as a figure appeared in the trees.

"Mac Bane," Nash announced, "you are under arrest."

The faint sounds of sirens wound through the air as Nash collapsed into a heap at the edge of the clearing.

NASH WOKE TO the blinding fluorescence of hospital lighting. His eyelids and limbs felt heavy and weak. His thoughts slow and muddled. The too-familiar scent of bleach and bandages reminded him of a thousand trips to see injured colleagues, witnesses and criminals.

The word *criminals* struck a chord, and his slitted eyes widened. "Lana."

A woman in a white physician's coat smiled at him. "Hello, Nash," she said. "You've had quite a day, I hear."

"Lana," he repeated with a voice that didn't sound like his own. Lana had been with Bane at the cabin. He'd thrown her down and pointed a gun at her.

Had Nash taken the shot?

The memory was fuzzy. The will to shoot had been there, but clarity had not. He'd been sure he'd die before he made it up the mountain.

"I'm Dr. Ward," the woman said. "Lana is fine." She swung a pointed finger toward the opposite side of the room.

Nash rolled his aching head to find Lana in the chair on his opposite side. Fresh tears rolled over her cheeks as she reached, speechless, for his hand.

He curled his fingers over hers. "I love you."

She made a sound that caught somewhere between a laugh and a sob, then bobbed her head. "I love you too." Her hair was pulled back, and her face was covered in cuts and bruises from their run through the dense woods. She was dressed in blue scrubs.

"Are you hurt?" he asked.

"No." She shook her head and tightened her hold on his fingers. "I'm okay. Because of you."

"You were shot," Dr. Ward interrupted, drawing Nash's attention back to her. "There was extensive damage to your femur, and you had surgery," she explained. "You lost a lot of blood, but you were lucky. I found an abundance of eager donors." She stepped aside, revealing the open door to his room behind her.

A dozen happy faces waited just outside. Half of them were Winchesters. "I'll let you visit for a while, but you have to tell me if you need a break. These folks don't seem the type to leave on their own or take a subtle hint."

Nash laughed, then winced at the pain in his thigh.

Dr. Ward turned a bemused expression on him as she stepped toward the little crowd. "You need to stay off that leg for at least six weeks. Eight would be better, but we can talk more about that later. For now, you need rest."

Nash nodded.

Dr. Ward's eyes flickered to Lana. "He'll need a lot of help for the first couple of weeks, and Winchesters aren't the type to accept it easily. I know. I've tended to more of them than you'd think."

The crowd chuckled.

"All right," Dr. Ward told the others, as she stepped into the hall. "Go on."

Aunt Rosa was the first to enter, eyes bright with relief as she rushed forward to kiss his forehead. Uncle Hank smiled proudly as he stood at her side.

Rosa patted his cheek. "I've called your mother. She's nearly here."

"Thank you," Nash said.

His cousin Isaac moved into position at his aunt and uncle's side. Then Knox with his new wife and baby.

Clusters of uniformed deputies and EMTs lingered in the hallway, allowing him time with family.

His teammate Victor was next through the door. His arm was in a sling, but he carried a smile on his face. "Craig and James are finishing the transport paperwork for Bane. They'll be here soon. We're all a little banged up, but we're alive, thanks to this guy." He turned to the door as he stepped aside.

Cruz pushed a wheelchair into the mix, with Derek as his passenger. "What can I say?" Cruz said. "I'm a hero."

Derek rolled his eyes. He wore a plain white T-shirt and gray sweat pants, but his head and hand were wrapped in gauze, and there seemed to be a bulky bandage beneath his shirt. "Allison's changing the baby," he said. "She'll be in when she finishes, so she can tell you what she thinks about me getting shot."

Nash grimaced at the number of injuries around him. Lana. His teammates. Now Derek? "You were shot?"

Lana squeezed Nash's hand. "I thought you were both dead," she said, voice thin and brittle. "I've never been so afraid."

Nash returned the squeeze, then fixed his eyes on Derek. "What happened?"

"I was on my way to the family cabin when the first shots rang out," Derek explained. "I turned around and went back, knowing you were under fire. I caught up with Bane pretty easily. That guy is not an outdoorsman." He shook his head, as if disappointed in the fugitive. "We tussled. I thought I had him, but his gun went off, and I rolled down the hill. I lost my gun and my phone in the fall. It took me forever to get back to the top. When I did, he was gone, and so were both of you. I headed back down the mountain to my car for the walkie-talkie to reach out to Knox and Cruz. By then, they were already on their way."

"Nash," Lana said, setting a gentle hand on his cheek, "you did it. You got Mac Bane."

The memory of firing on Mac was fuzzy but solidifying. "Did he live?"

He hoped so, because Bane needed to be prosecuted. Punished and jailed. This time, he wouldn't get away.

"He's stable," Derek said. "A deputy is posted outside his room. EMTs said he took two good hits."

"Heavens!" Aunt Rosa gasped. "You shot him twice?"

Isaac cleared his throat and rubbed a hand over his smiling lips. "Nash shot him once," he said. "Then Lana broke his tibia with a fallen tree limb."

Cruz mimed using a baseball bat. "I've told you. Your girl's got a ruthless swing."

Lana's cheeks darkened. A puff of laughter broke loose and spread across the crowd.

Nash pulled her hand to his lips. "You saved me," he said. "You dragged me to those rocks."

"You almost died," Lana answered, all signs of humor gone. "I thought I'd lost you."

"I'm right here," he told her. "And I'm not leaving again without your direct order."

Epilogue

Lana checked her fully completed task list for the tenth time, then her phone for messages. Unbelievable as it was, there was nothing left for her to do, and still no new messages.

It was hard to believe that after months of preparation, her new café would officially open tomorrow morning. Harder to believe, and infinitely more pressing, was the fact a jury was still out on the Mac Bane trial. The sequestered men and women had been deliberating for days but were expected to come to a decision tonight.

In some ways, it felt as if she hadn't taken a full breath since leaving Great Falls. Knowing Bane was captured but not yet convicted was more concerning than relieving. After all, he'd been a fugitive when he'd rolled into her life. He'd escaped custody once before.

"Lana?" Nash's voice broke through her reverie, pulling her eyes away from the phone. "How's this?" he called, over the merry notes of steel-drum music.

She'd hidden speakers throughout the dining area to add to the café's ambience.

Lana smiled as she took a moment to admire her handsome boyfriend, power drill in hand. He'd attached an old fishing net to the ceiling for atmosphere, and the result was delightful.

"Perfect."

The Island Vibes Café was going to be the go-to spot for affordable, accessible seafood and sushi in a casual, fun environment. A family-friendly hangout where everyone was welcome and well fed. Strategically positioned between Bellarmine University and the University of Louisville, Lana and all her favorite meals were about to become staples in the diets of thousands of college kids as well.

The decision to trade her life in Great Falls for a future with Nash in Louisville had been a no-brainer. He'd offered to move in with her while he healed, but she'd known the moment he'd been shot that life was too short and too fragile to waste. His work was in Louisville, and she could work anywhere, so she'd packed her things, and they'd traded his apartment for a rental home in the city.

Uncle Hank and Aunt Rosa chatted with Lana's parents at a large round table in the dining area's center, trading stories about life in Great Falls. Nash's parents interjected with anecdotes about Louisville, regularly encouraging both older couples to move to their town. The trio of elder couples had worked around the clock all week, helping prepare Island

Vibes for the grand opening, and providing silent support as Lana awaited the trial verdict.

Aunt Rosa and Uncle Hank had painted the café walls in a subtle ombré of blues, from navy to turquoise. They'd helped her parents frame and hang a collage of photos on the wall near the register. Dozens of old images of her dad's life growing up in Japan mixed with similar images of her mom's extended family in Hawaii. With Lana's lineage so visible in every detail of her café, she was sure she'd cook love into every dish.

Nash dropped the drill to his side and moved to meet her at the counter. "Everything looks amazing," he assured. "This place is going to be an enormous hit."

She smiled. "Your dad and Uncle Hank painted the dinghy from the flea market. Will you hang it next to the net?"

He pulled the trigger on the drill a few times, then kissed her on her forehead. "Point me to the dinghy."

She laughed and pointed.

Nash called for his dad's and uncle's help hoisting the old boat up a ladder. Then he began to attach the ceiling anchors.

Her mama turned in her seat at the table, catching Lana's eye. "Are the cakes ready?"

"Yes, ma'am." Lana smiled, then collected the tray of cooled Haupia cakes and toppings. Her future patrons were sure to fall in love with the coconut-milk-based pudding Lana used to layer the fluffy tiers, not to mention the creamy icing and generous amounts of shredded coconut her mother was about to put on top. "Here they are," she said, setting the extra-large tray on the table.

Her mama, Rosa and Nash's mother had insisted she bake and cook all day, preparing anything she could freeze or refrigerate for tomorrow. The sheer volume of ready product was borderline insanity, but the ladies were having so much fun helping, that the memories alone were worth the possibility of over-preparation.

The ladies' eyes widened, and Rosa looked to the sky, as if thanking the heavens for the sweetly scented cakes, or maybe praying for the strength not to eat one whole.

Lana had said both prayers a time or two as well.

Her mama dug into the work with gusto, an in-explicable expression of pride on her face. "Beautiful," she said, covering the stacked tiers in a smooth white gown of icing.

Nash joined Lana at the table, the dinghy secured perfectly overhead. "What do you think?" he asked the group.

The women looked up and grinned.

Her mom paused the icing efforts to raise a brow at Lana. "He's enthusiastic about your work. That's important."

Nash drew Lana close and kissed her head. "I'm enthusiastic about you in general."

The steel-drum melody changed, and her dad sashayed in their direction, one hand on his middle, the other reaching for her mama. His eyes danced as he pulled her from her seat and twirled her over the polished floorboards.

Nash's parents, aunt and uncle followed suit.

Nash's phone began to ring, and the room stilled.

The music quieted.

He placed his phone on the table, screen up, then quickly activated the speaker feature. "Winchester."

"Hey." Knox's voice rang through the line, and Rosa covered her mouth.

This was it.

Lana gripped Nash's arm.

He pulled her against his chest. "I'm with Lana, her folks and mine, plus Aunt Rosa and Uncle Hank," he said. "You're on Speaker. Tell me the jury came to a decision."

"Guilty on every count," Knox said.

The café erupted in cheers.

Lana felt the gasp rip from her throat, and a full, deep inhalation followed. Tim's and Heidi's families would at least have that closure.

Everyone else who'd been harmed during Bane's shooting spree, or by one of his hit men, had already fully recovered. The loan-sharking and money laundering operations in Great Falls had been thoroughly dismantled after Bane's arrest, and a few of the stooges he'd sent to find and kill Lana were attempting to make deals in exchange for leniency.

The nightmare was finally over.

"Lana," Knox said, pulling her attention back to the phone, "He'll be taken to a maximum security prison, where he's unlikely to ever get out."

She pressed her cheek against Nash's chest and wrapped him in her arms.

"And," Knox said, "the prosecution had a surprise witness. It seems Mitchell Edwards has been in protective custody since the day he ran. He was located and pulled from his boat before my men ever got there, and no one said a word. Apparently the trust circle is very small when it comes to Mac Bane."

"Mitchell's alive?" she asked, stunned and blinking back fresh tears.

"Yep. His testimony and yours were the biggest factors in the length of Bane's sentence. Mitchell will be free to return to his life in progress tomorrow. Apparently, he and Tim hosted regular boys' nights on the boat, where some serious money traded hands over poker. Bane got wind of the operation and wanted in. They said no, and they wouldn't reveal who played or where. Bane claimed Great Falls was his territory and accused them of overstepping. He planned to kill them both and pick up the poker nights where they left off."

Lana wiped falling tears from her cheeks. "Thank you so much for this news," she said, feeling suddenly lighter than she'd felt in far too long. "Are you still in town?"

Knox and his family had come to Louisville for

the trial, but it had been days since the attorneys had presented their closing arguments.

"We are," Knox said. "We were thinking of stopping by to congratulate you. Are you still at the café?"

Nash released her and headed for the front door.

"Yeah," she answered, watching curiously as the couples on the makeshift dance floor broke into action, heading for the business side of her counter and sliding tables together in the center of the floor.

Nash unlocked the front door and pushed it open wide.

A sea of familiar faces flooded inside, and the music rose once more.

Knox, Cruz, Derek, their wives and children, Isaac, Nash's teammates and a selection of Great Falls deputies, along with a dozen more Winchesters she recognized by face and name, but hadn't seen in years, greeted her with smiles and hugs.

She was passed from embrace to embrace as all the extra food she'd prepared was arranged buffet-style on the counter. It took several minutes for her to find her senses and look to Nash in explanation.

"I've been waiting for the trial to end," he said, taking her hand and moving in close. "I didn't want to do this while something so heavy hung over your shoulders."

She wrinkled her nose and scanned the suddenly silent crowd. "You planned this?"

"I had some help," he said, and the women behind the counter took bows.

Nash pulled a ring from his pocket and lowered onto his knee.

Her limbs shook and her heart pounded as the impossibility of having all her dreams come true at once became reality.

And when he asked, Lana said yes.

* * * * *

*Look for the previous books in
award-winning author Julie Anne Lindsey's
Heartland Heroes series:*

SVU Surveillance
Protecting His Witness
Kentucky Crime Ring
Stay Hidden
Accidental Witness

*You'll find them wherever
Harlequin Intrigue books are sold!*

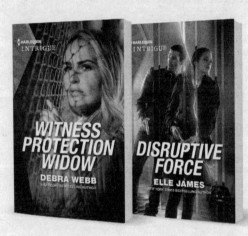

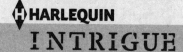
#2073 STICKING TO HER GUNS
A Colt Brothers Investigation • by B.J. Daniels
Tommy Colt is stunned when his childhood best friend—and love—
Bella Worthington abruptly announces she's engaged to their old-time nemesis!
Knowing her better than anyone, Tommy's convinced something is dangerously
wrong. Now Colt Brothers Investigations' newest partner is racing to uncover the
truth and ask Bella a certain question...if they survive.

#2074 FOOTHILLS FIELD SEARCH
K-9s on Patrol • by Maggie Wells
When two kids are kidnapped from plain sight, Officer Brady Nichols and his
intrepid canine, Winnie, spring into action. Single mother Cassie Whitaker thought
she'd left big-city peril behind—until it followed her to Jasper. But can Brady and
his K-9 protect Cassie from a stalker who won't take no for an answer?

#2075 NEWLYWED ASSIGNMENT
A Ree and Quint Novel • by Barb Han
Hardheaded ATF legend Quint Casey knows he's playing with fire asking
Agent Ree Sheppard to re-up as his undercover wife. To crack a ruthless Houston
weapons ring, they must keep the mission—and their explosive chemistry—under
control. But Quint's determined need for revenge and Ree's risky moves are
putting everything on the line...

#2076 UNDERCOVER RESCUE
A North Star Novel Series • by Nicole Helm
After the husband she thought was dead returns with revenge on his mind,
Veronica Shay resolves to confront her secret past—and her old boss,
Granger Macmillan, won't let her handle it on her own. But when they fall into a
nefarious trap, they'll call in their entire North Star family in order to stay alive...

#2077 COLD CASE CAPTIVE
The Saving Kelby Creek Series • by Tyler Anne Snell
Returning to Kelby Creek only intensifies Detective Lily Howard's guilt at the
choice she made years ago to rescue her childhood crush, Anthony Perez, rather
than pursue the man abducting his sister. But another teen girl's disappearance
offers a chance to work with Ant again—and a tantalizing new lead that could
mean inescapable danger.

#2078 THE HEART-SHAPED MURDERS
A West Coast Crime Story • by Denise N. Wheatley
Attacked and left with a partial heart-shaped symbol carved into her chest,
forensic investigator Lena Love finds leaving LA to return to her hometown comes
with its own danger—like detective David Hudson, the love she left behind.
But soon bodies—all marked with the killer's signature heart—are discovered in
David's jurisdiction...

*Wedding bells and shotgun fire are ringing out
in Lonesome, Montana. Read on for another
Colt Brothers Investigation novel from* New York Times
bestselling author B.J. Daniels.

Bella Worthington took a breath and, opening her eyes, finally faced her reflection in the full-length mirror. The wedding dress fit perfectly—just as he'd said it would. While accentuating her curves, the neckline was modest, the drape flattering. As much as she hated to admit it, Fitz had good taste.

The sapphire-and-diamond necklace he'd given her last night gleamed at her throat, bringing out the blue-green of her eyes—also like he'd said it would. He'd thought of everything—right down to the huge pear-shaped diamond engagement ring on her finger. All of it would be sold off before the ink dried on the marriage license—if she let it go that far.

As she studied her reflection, though, she realized this was exactly as he'd planned it. She looked the beautiful bride on her wedding day. No one would be the wiser.

She could hear music and the murmur of voices downstairs. He'd invited the whole town of Lonesome, Montana. She'd watched from the upstairs window as the guests had arrived earlier. He'd wanted an audience for this and now he would have one.

The knock at the door startled her, even though she'd been expecting it. "It's time," said a male voice on the other side. One of Fitz's hired bodyguards, Ronan, was waiting. He would be carrying a weapon under his suit. Security, she'd been told, to keep her safe. A lie.

She listened as Ronan unlocked her door and waited outside, his boss not taking any chances. He had made sure there was no possibility of escape short of shackling her to her bed. Fitz was determined that she find no way out of this. It didn't appear that she had.

In a few moments, she would be escorted downstairs to where her maid of honor and bridesmaids were waiting—all handpicked by her groom. If they'd questioned why they were down there and she was up here, they hadn't asked. He wasn't the kind of man women questioned. At least not more than once.

For another moment, Bella stared at the stranger in the mirror. She didn't have to wonder how she'd gotten to this point in her life. Unfortunately, she knew too well. She'd just never thought Fitz would go this far. Her mistake. He, however, had no idea how far she was willing to go to make sure the wedding never happened.

Taking a breath, she picked up her bouquet from her favorite local flower shop. The bouquet had been a special order delivered earlier. Her hand barely trembled as she lifted the blossoms to her nose for a moment, taking in the sweet scent of the tiny white roses—also his choice. Carefully, she separated the tiny buds, afraid it wouldn't be there.

It took her a few moments to find the long, slim silver blade hidden among the roses and stems. The blade was sharp, and lethal if used correctly. She knew exactly how to use it. She slid it back into the bouquet out of sight. He wouldn't think to check it. She hoped. He'd anticipated her every move and attacked with one of his own. Did she really think he wouldn't be ready for anything?

Making sure the door was still closed, she checked her garter. What she'd tucked under it was still there, safe, at least for the moment.

Another knock at the door. Fitz would be getting impatient and no one wanted that. "Everyone's waiting," Ronan said, tension in his tone. If this didn't go as meticulously planned, there would be hell to pay from his boss. Something else they all knew.

She stepped to the door and opened it, lifting her chin and straightening her spine. Ronan's eyes swept over her with a lusty gaze, but he stepped back as if not all that sure of her. Clearly he'd been warned to be wary of her. Probably just as she'd been warned what would happen if she refused to come down—or worse, made a scene in front of the guests.

At the bottom of the stairs, the room opened and she saw Fitz waiting for her with the person he'd hired to officiate.

He was so confident that he'd backed her into a corner with no way out. He'd always underestimated her. Today would be no different. But he didn't know her as well as he thought. He'd held her prisoner, threatened her, forced her into this dress and this ruse.

But that didn't mean she was going to marry him.

She would kill him first.

Don't miss
Sticking to Her Guns *by B.J. Daniels,*
available June 2022 wherever
Harlequin books and ebooks are sold.

Harlequin.com

After forensic investigator Lena Love is attacked and left with a partial heart-shaped symbol carved into her chest, her hunt to find a serial killer becomes personal.

Read on for a sneak preview of
The Heart-Shaped Murders,
the debut book in A West Coast Crime Story series,
from Denise N. Wheatley.

Lena Love kicked a rock out from underneath her foot, then bent down and tightened the twill shoelaces on her brown leather hiking boots.

The crime scene investigator, who doubled as a forensic science technician, stood back up and eyed Los Angeles's Cucamonga Wilderness trail. Sharp-edged stones and ragged shards of bark covered the rugged, winding terrain.

"Watch your step," she uttered to herself before continuing along the path of her latest crime scene.

Lena squinted as she focused on the trail. Heavy foliage loomed overhead, blocking out the sun's brilliant rays. She pulled out her flashlight, hoping its bright beam would help uncover potential evidence.

An ominous wave of vulnerability swept through her chest at the sight of the vast San Gabriel Mountains. She spun around slowly, feeling small while eyeing the infinite views of the forest, desert and snowy mountainous peaks.

The wild surroundings left her with a lingering sense of defenselessness. Lena tightened the belt on her tan suede blazer. She hoped it would give her some semblance of security.

It didn't.

Lena wondered if the latest victim had felt that same vulnerability on the night she'd been brutally murdered.

"Come on, Grace Mitchell," Lena said aloud, as if the dead woman could hear her. "Talk to me. Tell me what happened to you. *Show me* what happened to you."

A gust of wind whipped Lena's bone-straight bob across her slender face. She tucked her hair behind her ears and stooped down, aiming the flashlight toward the majestic oak tree where Grace's body had been found.

Lena envisioned spotting droplets of blood, a cigarette butt, the tip of a latex glove...*anything* that would help identify the killer.

This was her second visit to the crime scene. The thought of showing up to the station without any viable evidence yet again caused an agonizing pang of dread to shoot up her spine. Grace was the fifth victim of a criminal whom Lena had labeled an organized serial killer. He appeared to have a type. Young, slender brunette women. Their bodies had all been found in heavily wooded areas. Each victim's hands were meticulously tied behind their backs with a three-strand twisted rope. They'd been strangled to death. And the amount of evidence left at each scene was practically nonexistent. But the killer's signature mark was always there. And it was a sinister one.

Look for
The Heart-Shaped Murders by Denise N. Wheatley,
available June 2022 wherever
Harlequin Intrigue books and ebooks are sold.

Harlequin.com